Charon 1

By

A.H. Johnstone

www.ahjohnstone.com

COPYRIGHT © A. H. JOHNSTONE 2018

The Moral Rights of A. H. Johnstone to be recognised as the author of this work are asserted in accordance with the Copyright, Designs and Patents Act 1988.
All rights reserved.

No part of this may be reproduced, stored, transmitted, circulated or copied in any form or by any means without the consent of the author or an implied licence to do so.

This is a work of fiction.

Any references or resemblances to real people, events or locations are used fictitiously. Similarities to persons (living or dead) references people, events or locations referred to are coincidental and where real places have been used it has been for entirely artistic purposes and by no means implies endorsement of any kind, or any direct connection with the author.

ISBN: 978-198-3946-165
via CreateSpace

ACKNOWLEDGEMENTS

FORMATTING BY STEPHEN HUNT

COVER ART BY SARAH ANDERSON

EDITED BY MICHELLE DUNBAR, J. R O'BRYANT

A. H. Johnstone

CONTENTS

CHAPTER 1	7
CHAPTER 2	29
CHAPTER 3	47
CHAPTER 4	55
CHAPTER 5	73
CHAPTER 6	81
CHAPTER 7	97
CHAPTER 8	109
CHAPTER 9	123
CHAPTER 10	131
CHAPTER 11	137
CHAPTER 12	145
CHAPTER 13	169
CHAPTER 14	177
CHAPTER 15	183
CHAPTER 16	191
CHAPTER 17	197
CHAPTER 18	211

CHAPTER 19 223
CHAPTER 20 229
CHAPTER 21 239
CHAPTER 22 251
CHAPTER 23 263
CHAPTER 24 273
CHAPTER 25 289
CHAPTER 26 305

Rules of The Council and the Conditions of The Settlement of the Gods. 329

The Rules of the Council............................ 331
Conditions of Settlement............................ 335

Upcoming 339

The Bet 341

Notes and references to the more obscure deities... 353

CHAPTER 1

The Meeting

Charon swore. The monitor he had been battling with for the last hour had flickered off yet again. There was a pop from under the desk followed by the smell of burnt plastic. 'Typical.' He groaned as he crawled under the desk and fought with the mass of wire. Eventually, he found the correct lead and followed it to the power socket. The plug had melted. Struggling to his feet he picked up the telephone and hit one of the autodial keys.

'Yes. It's the front desk. Again. Put me through to IT please. Quick as you like. It's not as though any of us have work to do or anything.' He waited for ten minutes on hold, listening to a very tinny, off-tempo, instrumental version of *Rhinestone Cowboy*. It played on a loop, accompanied by Charon grinding his teeth.

A curse on the demon who came up with this damnable tune... A crackling line broke him off mid-thought. Finally, someone answered. The voice at the other end was muffled.

'This is IT. I hear you have a problem. Sorry to hear that. Can I ask you the nature of your problem, and I will put you through to the right department?'

'For the tenth time this week, you mean? You keep a record of calls, don't you?'

'Yes, sir, but it might be a different prob—'

'For the last time, my security monitor has finally burned out. I've been chasing you lot for new ones for weeks.'

'I'm sorry to hear that, sir. Would you like to visit our website and complete the customer satisfaction survey?'

'No, I would not! I work for this company, I am not a *customer*!'

'Sorry to hear that but—'

'I don't want to hear how sorry you are! I want it

fixed or replaced, or whatever in seven Hells you lot bloody do all day! Today!' he snapped.

'Well I'm sorry but we have to prioritise our attention where it can be most profitably invested,' he whined. It sounded almost like he had a peg on his nose, 'maintenance of hired equipment is not our problem...'

'Not your problem, huh?' he sighed, 'Exactly what is your problem? I mean we appear to have an IT department who won't do any IT. At least not beyond telling me to turn it off and back on again. When you can eventually be pressed to send an engineer, there is never one available on the day and when they are they never appear. You do seem to have plenty of your 'Sorry you were out' cards which magically appear all by themselves.' The voice, however indistinct, seemed extremely familiar to him. Charon found himself flexing an otherwise innocent biro to near breaking point. He was about to hurl it across the foyer before he realised he'd only have to go and get it. The voice probably knew him too and was, therefore, doing this on purpose and probably found it extremely funny. Should he keep it to himself?

'Oh, bugger this!' Charon hadn't meant to say that out loud but centuries of keeping to himself had led him into a habit of thinking aloud or rehashing conversations he had wished had lasted longer, just for the company.

'Sir! Please moderate your...'

'Hermes? Is that you?' He hadn't seen his friend in nearly a century. Since being dragged from the Underworld to the back of beyond to guard the foyer of one officially disused office block after another, he hadn't seen much of anyone. It was dull, but he didn't complain. Who would he complain to? It paid and there was relatively little actual work to do. Weekends off too. There was a clatter at the other end of the line.

'What?' his shock was audible, 'How do you know my name? Who told you?' *Paranoid as ever; some things never change.*

'It's me, Herm. It's Charon. How did you end up on an IT helpdesk?' he laughed.

'Charon? Well, I'll be damned!'

Charon thought Hermes probably should have reconsidered that expression given who he was speaking to.

Hermes continued sulkily, 'I am only on the telephone communications side of it. They won't let me near any actual equipment. My presence seems to fry it.' Hermes sounded deflated. 'My other role is far less exciting. I am also a bicycle courier, though not by choice. It was a punishment for something. Can't remember what I did now. Deadlines don't seem to be the forte of our 'employers'. Eternity or nothing.'

How droll, Charon thought. It was remarkable how little imagination their masters had. Even before they came here, and they still had their full powers, the gods could be quite creative in their petty vindications. They were still petty, capricious and vindictive but, now faced with modernity, they'd become downright dull; if not lazy. Before he had been forced to manifest into human form, he had been little more than a creepy doorman. Once sucked out of the twisted collective imaginations of these bipedal apes, he was transplanted into the nearest appropriate human body and put back to work... as a security guard. As an abstract, he couldn't just manifest, so he'd been shoved into a random mortal. No bespoke form for him, oh no. Aside from bodies and scenery, not a lot had changed.

The only difference he'd noticed since he stopped ferrying the dead across that river to Hades seemed to be that the boat had gone and his feet stayed dry. *River? Stinking bog was more like it.* Now he had the freedom to move around as he pleased but that was more due to the limit of their powers than any special consideration on their part and he could still find himself in serious trouble if he let the wrong person through those doors. Once he had been chained up as punishment for 'letting' Heracles beat him up and get past him. *For a hero, that boy's moral compass had been way off. Maybe he had a magnet in his pocket?'* Charon nearly choked from laughing when Heracles changed the spelling of his name to something more 'contemporary'. They'd nearly all gone along with the mortals and 'Romanised' their names, but Charon had suspected Heracles' decision had a lot to do with the long standing spat between him and his stepmother. She hated the boy and the feeling was mutual. He shook his head. Back to the point. 'Hermes. Buddy. Can you please send me an engineer? I have about three hours before a load of the shiny-arses arrive for some big meeting and if the 'wrong people' wander in, I am for it.'

'Who are the 'wrong people'?'

'Who do you think? Mortals. *Lesser* beings', beings with a pulse and a birth certificate or anyone not currently in someone's good books. You know what they're like. Who can keep up?

'Oh, them,' Hermes paused, 'do any of them really believe in us anymore? Most of them look at me like I have given them a headache.' Hermes had been able to manifest which meant mortals couldn't quite focus on him or fix his face in their heads. Zeus was not happy about it either. For a being that had spent hundreds of years pretending to be other people and creatures - mostly for the purpose of getting into as many pairs of knickers as he could manage while not getting caught by the Mrs - it had surprised Charon that his new inconspicuous incarnation had raised such consternation. He'd had to wonder about the one seduced by a swan...

'Not enough of the old stories about us survive to

give a real boost to whatever belief is keeping us here, at least not anymore. There are a few oddballs and the academic sort who think that we were 'literary constructs of mortal experiences'. The Fae Courts and The Council like to keep us as quiet as possible. Something about abiding by the same set of conditions everyone signed when we came over. Basically, we've got the power we came with and it's going to have to last us. Strictly no top-ups allowed' Charon said.

The Council was made up of the Norns[i], the Fates, the Furies etc. Basically, every group of abstracts deemed capable of getting the head gods to simmer down and behave themselves. The Muses had been kicked off some time ago for allegedly inspiring some rather unpleasant business involving an otherwise harmless vicar and a militant seagull, though nothing was officially proven…

'I didn't sign anything.' Hermes snorted back a laugh, 'Who's coming for this one?'

'The biggest bullies in the playground of course,' it disgusted Charon that thousands of years of loyalty, albeit reluctant, wouldn't merit a more senior role. He wasn't surprised. Then again, he didn't know what he would do with new responsibility, he just knew he wanted it. He considered approaching Hades again next time he was in. 'Come on, Herm, do it for a mate.'

'Because it's you, I'll see what I can muster up. In return, you can meet me in that pub on the corner near your building. Oh, and you're buying. TTFN.' Hermes hung up.

'TTFN? Whatever next?' He looked around the foyer. It depressed him. Once it had shone. Gleamed even. Now the smell of damp permeated through the whole building. The once brilliant matte white walls were streaked with mould, dust and mildew where the roof and window seals had leaked. The chrome coatings on the barriers and bannisters were flaking and corroded, and the floor was covered in a carpet of cracked linoleum tiles, dead leaves, and the litter which had blown in from the playing field behind the building through a hole in the now boarded window panel. Added to this there was the smell of damp plaster everywhere he went.

He decided to kill time and at least get rid of the

rubbish. As he swept he looked down at his faded black uniform with the printed grey badge reading 'Ferryman Security'. It was flaking. Decaying like everything else they had a hand in. Something about their influence in the mortal world was toxic. He'd just put the broom away when a black van – he assumed it was black, but the dirt made it hard to tell – pulled up in front of the main doors. He went out to investigate. Before he could launch into his well-rehearsed 'You can't park that there, mate' routine' the driver leapt out, flashed him an ID, a fanged grin, and then slid open the side door of the vehicle.

'Herm said he owed you one. Where do you want this lot? You'll have to sign for it.' He handed Charon a clipboard with one black-nailed, and slightly orange tinged hand, and indicated the boxes of equipment behind him with the other.

* * *

Within two hours Charon had a brand-new security system complete with intercom and automated doors. That demon had worked like, well, a demon. No human could have worked at that speed. Hermes had earned that pint. Maybe he should have offered the technician a cup of tea, but he was one of Arawn's crew and that lot gave him the creeps. The Underworld held perils in its belly, but *they* were a law unto themselves and everyone steered clear. Even Cerberus started whimpering and tucked his tail in when that lot were about. Charon did help him pack up his van but only so he would be gone as quickly as possible. He checked the time again. Twenty minutes to spare.

When people began to arrive, Charon trudged through his assigned script. It wasn't hard. Ask the Name. Check the list for the name. Make them sign the visitors' log, issue a badge, and give directions to the upstairs lounge. Some of them were not quite as omnipresent as they liked to pretend, so he'd had to show several how to operate the lifts. *Surely, they could have worked out lifts by now, but then they have only been here for a millennium. Why hurry?*

They still acted like gods, but thanks to a frankly ridiculous punch up, and a very misguided wine fuelled bet, had found themselves begging for asylum in the mortal world. All they had left was to hang around and wait for the last of the memories to fade. This had been Yahweh's idea of an easy way to get shot of all of them. *And wasn't he just as pleased as Punch? Turned up to make sure we all crossed over without a hitch too. And he made sure we saw Gabriel and another of his lackeys measuring up for a refit...Git!* He never could tolerate competition. What Yahweh hadn't banked on was the way their stories had seeped into the cultures they now inhabited. Drama, poetry and prose had provided at least some of them an anchor to cling to. Holding them here whether they wanted to stay or not.

Charon looked through the list again. There was no sign of the organiser's name, but all the names had one thing in common. They were all the head of their respective pantheons and their presence did not bode well. Gods, former or otherwise, only gathered like this if there was big trouble, and only if the Council had approved it. He was perplexed that Zeus, Hades and Poseidon had *all* been invited while Odin's name had been scrubbed off the list by a very angry hand. This struck Charon as odd, but he thought no more of it. It wasn't his job to ask questions, just keep his head down and do the job.

Don't get involved. Getting 'involved' got people killed. He'd seen enough before the pass to tell him that much. Charon wondered what force could have had the influence to have pulled them all to a rundown office block in High Wycombe? Then it dawned on him. Officially, they were supposed to be keeping a low-profile and not attracting attention, so it was a good idea for them to maintain an appearance of absence. Setting up a base in a small, grey, industrial town just outside London that most of the country hadn't heard of either was a damned sure-fire way of achieving that.

Just as Charon was deciding over whether to attempt to get the kettle working, 'He' arrived. The 'Lord without limits'. With a full entourage. None of whom were on his list. *That's just great.* He pressed the door release and stood in front of the desk to properly greet him. 'Ra, I had no idea you were coming. You did not appear on the list they gave me...'

'Charon, you know better than that. I do not need to make people aware I am coming. It somewhat spoils the surprise, don't you think?' he chided, gently. 'The sun always comes.' His voice was soft.

Not deep, but quiet and smooth. His mortal form had somehow become the mortal embodiment of his former self. His dark skin shimmered with gold flecks and reflected a gold glow into the dark foyer. In the right light, it was uncomfortable to look at him directly. Charon wasn't certain that this characteristic was entirely accidental given Ra's predilection for glamour and glitz.

'Can I lead you up to the meeting room, sir?' Charon hoped he refused. He only knew a fraction of what was in those offices and he didn't want to know about the rest. He had been explicitly warned not to venture past the third floor…

'No. Thank you. I know where I need to be. Am I the first to arrive?'

Charon tried not to make his relief visible. 'No, sir. According to my list there are still some yet to arrive, and some have not responded.'

Ra did not seem at all surprised or even interested by this. Charon continued, 'I have sent them up to the second-floor lounge, as per the instruction. Let me assure you that Odin has not attended.'

'That is because I did not invite him. He is... not reliable when it comes to matters requiring discretion.' He waved his entourage away. 'Can I be sure of your own, Charon?'

'Sir?'

'Yes, of course. You are not as loose with your words as some of your kind. Was there something else you wished to ask me? I am very busy.'

'I was wondering, if it's not presumptuous of me, but what happened to Aken? I don't see him here.'

'Sadly, he has already faded. His stories were not as strong or well known as your own. There was no anchor for him here. He vanished almost as soon as he left the shores of the Nun. Oh, well. He was never the best conversationalist. We barely notice his absence. I dare say we manage quite well without him.'

Charon said nothing but his heart sank. He considered whether this was the whole truth. Aken had been his equal, and a firm friend. He should have made it over. Ra had managed to bring that damned barque through the pass and secure bodies for his nearest and dearest, *Why not Aken?* It stung to hear him so easily disregarded.

Even the Olympians had found a way for Charon to pass through safely, though he suspected that came more out of a desire to not have to train another servant than any consideration for his wellbeing on their part. He decided to mourn Aken later as his grief would not be well received here. Ra waited at the lift for someone to press the button for him. One of his own attendants scurried over and obliged, bowing and scraping. It was pathetic, because in mortal form - gold infused skin and eyes aside - Ra looked like every other modern western businessman. Just more so. It was this that The Council meant by 'drawing undue attention'. Ra entered the lift and gave Charon the barest of courteous nods. As soon as the lift doors closed, the previously prim and orderly attendants began whipping out magazines and cigarettes and calling lounge furniture out of thin air. This just would not do.

'Oi! You! Yes, you, with the horns and the flashy green coat. Put that out or go outside!' The demon scowled at him and mooched out into the drizzle, pointedly allowing the door to slam behind it. The door shook in the frame and the diagonal crack in one corner grew another inch. Charon turned to the room at large. 'Can you please *not* do that thing with the furniture? There are cameras in here. How am I supposed to explain to the Council why the foyer was suddenly changed into what can at best be described as a Turkish harem in full view of the public?'

'Not our problem, chummy. While his nibs is up there, we might as well be comfortable down here.' He made himself comfortable on a long chaise, upholstered in gold Damask. It was quite a sight. 'I reckon he doesn't even realise we still exist when he's swanning off on his jollies.' Some of the others grumbled their agreement then returned to their card game. Charon saw their point. Hades pretty much ignored him until he wanted something too.

Charon sighed. 'Fine. Just keep the noise down. I have work to do.' Arguing seemed pointless. This lot just didn't care. He stomped off toward the kitchenette for a fresh cup of tea. From the back of the room he heard another click of a cheap lighter, 'And smoke outside!' he shouted without turning around to see who it was. Charon considered asking them to at least tone the room down to a milder level of... what was the best descriptor? He fished around his memory for something that would adequately cover the level of tasteless extravagance currently in his lobby but decided that the concept of 'subtlety' wouldn't register with them anyway. *What was wrong with grey? Wasn't monochrome the height of fashion again or some such nonsense?*

His thoughts were again interrupted by the arrival of the stragglers who demanded that he escort them up himself. *It's something to do I suppose.* He stood by the lift buttons and held the doors open. As they went up he pondered again why Zeus *and* his brothers had been invited. Zeus was never one to share power either, and Charon would have paid his weight in gold to see Zeus's face when he received a summons to assemble. Hades too. *Those three and their 'honour'.* A being like Ra ordering them about was going to grate on their nerves and the results would be entertaining to say the least.

The only other beings brave enough to issue orders to those three were the Council. That was a thought. *Where are the Council reps?* If the Council hadn't called this meeting, did they even know about it? They were supposed to be notified of all cross-pantheon meetings so they could send a representative.

After he'd escorted the stragglers to the right room, he switched on the cameras in that room and listened in from the second-floor reception desk. Their bickering would be something to laugh over with Hermes later and he was quite looking forward to that pint now. Ra had not gone in yet – he was still preening in the wall mirror outside the conference room - but Charon would bet money he was listening to every word they said before he went in. He was waiting to make as showy an entrance as possible.

Sure enough, Ra went for showy. Both doors opened at once and he strolled in with one hand in his pocket, his shirt sleeves rolled to the elbow and his jacket hooked on one finger over his shoulder. He reminded Charon of a 1980s' catalogue model.

'Gentlemen, Ladies. Welcome. Have we all arrived? Splendid.' The room was packed. Every chair around a dust covered meeting table had been taken and those who had not arrived on time to take a seat hovered behind, shifting their weight from foot to foot, and trying hard not to look impatient.

'Why have we been dragged here, Ra? We are not puppets to have our strings pulled! You know the law. Only the Council has the authority to summon us like this,' a gravelly voice demanded. Its owner, Zeus, occupied the chair at the head of the long table and was leaning back, with his expensive loafer-clad feet on the table. Ra ignored the deliberate insult of refusing to give up his seat to an older god. It wasn't the law, but it had long been custom to show respect to the elders of other Pantheons.

Charon held his breath as Ra sauntered across the floor between the hoard of irritable gods and the algae encrusted window. He clearly enjoyed holding the attention of the room.

'I quite understand.' His voice remained calm and level. He gave a half smile which did not meet his eyes. 'I know very well who each of you are and where your loyalties lie. I am also certain that you need no introductions to one another.' He walked to the window. 'I am sorry to disappoint you, but grudges and scores will not be dealt with here or now.' Staring out over the field to watch the train pass in the distance. 'I invite you here for one reason alone; to give you notice to tidy your affairs. Settle your arguments and make what peace you can before we leave. I have found a way home.'

A. H. Johnstone

CHAPTER 2

The Pub

The room erupted with concerned complaints.

Outside and down the corridor, Charon frowned at the monitor. It was an awkward angle to observe from. All he could see were the tops of peoples' heads which meant he couldn't see their expressions. He turned up the volume on the earpiece he was wearing.

'What are you blathering about, Ra?' The same gravelly voice as before cut through a chorus of voices all trying to drown out the others.

Ra turned his emotionless pale gold eyes on the speaker and then observed the rest of the table shrink back from him. Hades, who was lounging back in his chair paring his nails, raised an eyebrow at this pointed scrutiny, 'Let our friend speak, brother. His presumption is proving most entertaining.'

'Friend? He is no friend of mine! He is a pretender; all pomp but no substance. He is no better than the foul usurper who stole our homes and sent us here to rot'

'Well, this 'pretender' is tired,' Ra replied calmly. He sounded almost bored. Like what he said was of no real consequence to any of them. Even Charon was shocked. One thing he was sure about was that the Council had most definitely *not* approved this meeting! Zeus had confirmed that much. Should he tell them? If they found out and he hadn't told them there would be hell to pay. He stared back at the security screen trying to stop his hands shaking and heart racing.

'Pardon? You bring us all the way here because you are...'tired'?' the sibilant voice of Quetzalcoatl asked. 'What does this have to do with us? Has it not occurred to you that some of us travelled quite some distance to get here? We expect a lot more in the way of explanation than that.' The camera view switched angles and Charon saw his face. He was still recognisable. The feathers might be gone but there was still something snake-like about him in the eyes and nose. It gave him the creeps.

'In short, I intend to fulfil my promise to Osiris. The earth will return to its primordial form, the lands will flood, and I shall take my place by his side as Amun. You have a year to tidy your affairs, inform your subordinates, and prepare yourselves to leave this realm.'

'What of the mortals?' someone asked from the back of the room.

'What of them?' Ra shrugged. 'I understand that a few of you have made yourselves very comfortable here, even become fond of them, and it is unfortunate that they will become collateral damage, but this will only work once. It's one out, all out, and I place rather more importance on my survival than theirs. That is all.' With that, he left the room. There was dead silence while the door was left to close quietly behind him.

Charon had heard every word and having watched the exchange on the security monitor, knew Ra was coming so ducked behind the desk. This would mean the end of this realm. Not just gods but mortals too. He did not want to be caught eavesdropping, but this news was grave indeed. He needed more than a pint to deal with this news. This exit seemed a little anti-climactic to Charon. After delivering news like that the least Ra could have offered was a good hard door slam.

* * *

It was coming up to eight in the evening. Charon sat nursing his sixth pint in two hours and was considering giving up and going home. The pub was silent bar the faint noise from the traffic outside, and the quiet chink of glasses behind the bar. Charon sat at a table which gave him a clear view of the door and had waited there for the better part of two hours. He'd been staring into space for the duration and was beginning to get funny looks from the barman. The pub was one of those normally only frequented by old men and people who drank before lunchtime, with décor that suggested that it hadn't been updated since 1970. The door opened letting in a burst of traffic noise and cold wind. Charon peered over his narrow glasses, ready to give a menacing scowl to the inconsiderate sod who was letting all the warm air out. It wasn't Hermes. *If he's not here in the next ten minutes, I am going home… via the chippy.* He pulled his coat tighter around his shoulders and thought of chunky chips with gravy, and crispy, golden batter while he waited for the pub to get warm again.

Hermes arrived in the nick of time in his usual, disgustingly happy mood.

'What time do you call this?'

'About eight o'clock, bud. Why, what time do you call it?'

'I call it you being late.' Charon downed the rest of his pint and stomped off to the bar to get his friend a drink as well as a new one for himself.

When he returned Hermes looked at him, as if trying to spot signs of an imposter. It was quite unnerving to be looked at by Hermes. For a start he didn't blink, ever. Whether it was something he had never gotten the hang of, or he hadn't bothered to learn, it gave Charon chills. It was too much like facing one of the souls he'd had to carry across the Styx so long ago. Only this one was chatty.

'What? Look, can you not do that!?'

Hermes didn't stop. 'Bud, you're as white as a sheet, I mean, more than normal.'

'I used to be a mythically animated skeleton. I would have thought that this is an improvement.' He spread his hands and gestured to his very human body.

'True. What's the matter?'

'I listened in.'

While clearing up the beer Hermes had sprayed over the table, Charon explained what happened at the meeting, who was there, what was said, and even how he'd had to hide behind the second-floor security desk to dodge Ra.

'Well, that's a surprise. I'd never have taken you for such a daredevil.' Hermes grinned.

'What? Is that all you can say?'

'You've always been Mr Follow the Rules to my knowledge. Have you got any idea what Ra would have done if you had been caught? He doesn't mess around. One step wrong and it's...' Hermes drew one finger across his throat.

'He calls himself 'Ray' here.'

'And?'

'Hermes, what is the worst he could do to me? He has no authority here, at least not over me. It's in 'The Rules'. You know, the same ones that said none of us may undo the works of another, though I have always thought that was a stupid rule. I think Zeus just made that one up to be aggravating. Anyway, that's not the point.'

'No?'

'We're talking about the end of the world here. You, me, humanity, everyone. I think this is slightly more important than whether that preening adolescent spotted me eavesdropping. Look who was at the meeting.' He pulled out a crumpled photocopy of the original list. Hermes stared at it in his usual disconcerting way.

'I've got to be honest, bud, I just don't see the link.'

Charon sighed. Persuading Hermes to grasp the

gravity of a situation had always been a challenge. Information appeared to be flowing from ear to brain at roughly the speed of custard. This was going to take some time. 'Despite the rules, Ra only invited those who don't have the power or influence to stop him. Even back when we were at the height of our influence, Ra could beat or match everyone on that list.' He jabbed at the paper in front of him with one grey finger.

'You make it sound like some divine game of Top Trumps' Hermes laughed until he saw the familiar faint blue glow behind Charon's impassive blue eyes. The one that told him that he was skating on some very thin ice.

'Can you be serious for five minutes? Just try, hmm? Anyway, these guys no longer have the strength of collective belief behind them they used to, and look, Odin's been scrubbed off. See. Here?' He pointed at the hastily highlighted line which had been scrubbed out by hand. 'Why?'

'Off the top of my head? Odin pissed him off. Besides he and the Aesir have never had time for Ra's lot. Maybe he objected to being summoned and told Ra where to shove his invitation.'

'Could be,' Charon stared at the remains of his pint. It didn't make sense. *Why now?* Ra had seemed content to live among the mortals for centuries. Why would he suddenly be discontent? He'd been as rich as Midas since he had managed to orchestrate the looting of his own temples and monuments. Of course, he'd been extremely careful to make sure it didn't all go back to his own vaults, not directly at any rate. *Vaults? Who needs more than one?* Ra's reasoning had been that since the money and treasures had already been dedicated to him, they were technically his to take. It wasn't like he was taking the offerings to other gods.

'Why are you so worried, Charon?'

'Because if Ra is permitted to do this, the whole human plane of existence goes with it. Kaput. Poof! Gone! He said it can only be done once so it's probably devastating.'

'Surely you are not attached to the meat puppets? Zeus made them because he was bored and needed something to exorcise his frustrations. Though, personally, I believe Prometheus's side of it.' He laughed. 'Zeus was only angry because Prometheus thought of it first but giving them fire then sitting back to see what they did with it? Comic genius! Aristophanes himself could not have done better!'

'Why should I not be?' Charon snapped, 'It was me that had to ferry them to their end. Not all of them were happy to go, either, and I got them all you know, the murderers and murdered, the infants who didn't survive birth and those who were abandoned on hillsides. I saw the worst and the best. For puppets, they have potential.'

'I know what you saw, I had to take them to meet you, remember, it's how we met? Surely, that should be enough to make you wash your hands of them?'

'They grew. *They learned.* It's us that didn't change. Now, for the most part, they care for their young and their vulnerable.'

'Not all of them.'

'No, not all, but enough. They were never our puppets anyway, no matter what Zeus and Prometheus claim. They're both liars in that respect. They evolved despite us, not because of us. A balance for our own immortality. The creator gods might take the credit for them, but they never would acknowledge their own limitations because their egos would never allow it. They know as well as we do that the mortal life forms were an unknown quantity[ii]. They just know that most of us don't have the guts to contradict them.'

'Go on?' Hermes sat back in his chair and folded his arms. He was clearly not buying his line of argument.

Charon pressed on, 'How many times have they tried to destroy them[iii] and remake them for some slight or other?'

'More times than I can count.' Hermes took another swig. 'Is this going somewhere?'

'I'm getting there,' Charon glowed at him again.

'Okay, okay, carry on.'

'Thank you. One question seemed to irk Zeus more than any other. Why would any of the so-called creator gods create flawed beings only to punish them for the flaws they were created with?'

'Your point being? The creator gods are a bunch of petulant kids! How long has it taken you to work that one out?

'My point is that even that psycho, Yahweh, had to come up with excuses as to why his favoured creations were not behaving.'

'Well, he never was quite right in the head, that one. A bit too starry if you ask me. Inclined to stand that little bit too close and, by gods, did he get touchy if he thought someone was treading on his turf without his say so. There we all were, sitting pretty until some bleeding Roman wins a battle, and suddenly, we are *all* out on our arses. Who made that bridge bet?'

'Dionysus, it was a messy night, but it wasn't as simple as that and you know it.' Charon said. 'If I remember rightly, you were there too, egging them on. It was right before Dionysus headbutted Baal.'

'Was that the night when…?'

'When you and Di got stinking drunk with a pair of nymphs and decided to go skinny-dipping in the Styx… Yes, it was.'

'Yeah, well Yahweh wound us up, and the others are just plain scary. Some of those saints aren't all that saintly either. Ra will be doing us and them a massive favour by getting us home and I will be first in line to punch Yahweh in the face.'

'Will he really be doing you a favour too, old friend? And nobody is going to be punching anyone!'

'Okay. Some of them are a laugh, I suppose but this eternity thing is just getting boring. I am still stuck doing the same job as before. So are you, for that matter, but the creepy doorman thing seems to suit you.'

'Thanks.' Charon said.

'You're welcome. Look, neither of us has the power we used to have, and even my helm has stopped working. The best I can manage now is vaguely translucent and so much for my speed. I had one role then, and one role now, and it's dull. I've had enough.'

'The Council put a block on your helmet because you were using it to spy on the Vestal virgins in the shower.' He took a slow swig of beer. 'You might not see the point, but I can't let Ra make that choice for us all. It must be a group decision. His time has been and gone. I don't get why he can't just go back on his own? It's always all or nothing with him. Another thing to remember Herm, is that when we were in our powers, *you* had the freedom to move around and have your own life. Not all of us did, and some of us are not ready to leave the party. We have to stop him.'

'What are you proposing?' Hermes frowned. 'Just supposing for one delusory moment that you even managed to figure out a way to stop him, what about the rest of us? You can't just speak for us all any more than Ra can.' Hermes sat quietly for a moment, 'I'm tired too, dude. Never ageing or changing, and not being able to stay anywhere for more than ten years or people start asking awkward questions, having to keep our heads down all the time. Not to mention the lies and the secrets we need just to maintain a believable backstory.' Hermes finished his sixth pint and signalled the barman for another two, ignoring the disapproving expression of the student with the spiky green hair behind the bar. He seemed both amazed that either of them was still upright, let alone sober, and disgusted that he was expected to do something other than play with his phone.

'I get it, Charon, I really do, but I can't carry on like this much longer either. I'll probably take my chances and head off when the opportunity comes but assuming that Ra quits - which won't happen without a fight - *and* if you somehow get Ra to spare you and the mortals, and anyone else who wants to stay, what happens when you *do* decide you have had enough? What if there really is no way back for you? Look, I need another pint and that barman doesn't seem to get the idea of table service. Want one?' Charon nodded his silent agreement.

While Hermes went to the bar Charon considered what he had said. He had no intention of forcing anyone to stay who did not want to, but he didn't see why it had to mean the end of the world. Ra had no right to decide for them but he had not considered that there might be consequences for stopping Ra either. It could well be a go now or stay forever situation, but was it? There were too many questions which just led to other questions. He racked his brains trying to remember the actual wording of Ra's promise. It prophesied the world being swallowed by the ocean or some such melodramatic nonsense. He moved on to the next part of the prophecy.

'After I change myself back into a serpent...' he muttered.

'What was that?' Hermes had returned to their table and was taking a long swig from his fresh pint. 'Can you believe the price of this stuff? Where is Dionysus when you need him!?'

'I was just trying to remember the exact wording of the promise. It's been so long.'

'Well that's a relief, I thought you had flipped.'

'Something about him changing back to his true 'unseeable' form. Does that mean invisible or just that no man was worthy to look at him? Damn! Why do they always have to speak in riddles?'

'Kicks. It confuses the hell out of the mortals and *that* is always fun.'

'Well, it definitely mentions the end of creation, that means all of us, and knowing Ra it will be messy... and painful.' Charon was thinking aloud now.

'What does this have to do with our current problem?'

'It means that if we know what he has planned then he *is* stoppable.' Charon said.

'Working on the assumption that we *want* to stop him. And when did this become a 'we' situation?'

'Back on that again are *we*? I think he can be stopped, and it goes back to this list. You might be right. We might not be able to stop him, but we may be able to persuade him to adjust his plan.'

'To what?'

'To only go himself, or only take those who are willing to go with him by their own choice.'

'This is the head honcho of the Egyptian pantheon. One of the oldest mythical families on record. We must do as he says. By age alone they outrank us--'.

'Ah, but according to the rules of the council, they *don't* outrank us. He is bound by the same rules we are. This is probably why he hasn't bothered to let the Council know.'

'Ra's as likely to change his mind as Zeus is to join a hippy commune. Remember what that lot used to demand of their slaves?'

'I have to try. The worst he can do is sling me out of his office. He's survived for this long so he must get the idea of negotiation.'

They stared at each other across the table. Charon knew he hadn't persuaded Hermes that even attempting to stop Ra was in any way a good idea. Could he even be certain he had his friend's support in his desire to make Ra's plan at least a little less devastating?

CHAPTER 3

The First Warning

The door slammed shut behind him as Charon shed his coat and threw his key into the bowl by the door. He flicked the lights on and the room was filled with a dingy yellow-brown light. *Christ*, he thought, *this place is a dump*. Every surface was covered with the general detritus of life; unopened post, ancient copies of the Racing Post and screwed up betting slips, and clean laundry yet to be put away, but he was never the domestic type. Ever since Hel, the former queen of Nilfheim, had upped and left him, he'd just not seen the point. Why bother clearing up, when he had no one to share the space with? He'd told her every day that he loved her but had realised all too late that words are not enough. He had no neighbours, no one to miss him or even complain about how he always slammed the front door behind him.

One of the many drawbacks of being a lower level deity in the mortal world was that the higher-ups still got to boss him around. When they'd been made to cross over, the higher-ranking gods had insisted that the living conditions of their mortal forms should reflect their previous stations. There was to be no social-climbing for them, oh no. In fairness, Hades had eventually spoken for him and the Council had reluctantly allowed Charon to pick a human form to live on the surface on the provision that he didn't tell anyone else or all the Underworld denizens would want one. Living rent free was all well and good but why did it have to be here? He was luckier than those lower down than him. Many of them had never seen daylight. He felt a pang of regret then for Aken. Had Hades not spoken up he would have suffered the same fate.

He couldn't really see much of a difference between his situation then and what he had to put up with now though. He was still stuck working for Hades, and through him, Zeus. Every time he'd tried to move on and got a job offer elsewhere, a few days later, a letter would arrive saying they were sorry that he had chosen to decline their offer, but should he decide to apply again in the future, they would be delighted to hear from him. He had suspected Hades had a hand in that but couldn't prove it.

Now he was stuck in an abandoned Victorian terrace in the shadow of the railway bridge. Like the Styx, it was cold, dank, smelled weird, and had things growing on the walls that didn't bear thinking about. Even when Hel was with him he'd not been great at the domestic side of things. He'd just left it for Hel, he'd just assumed she would be happy to run around picking up after him. How he'd taken her for granted. No wonder she had left him. Even after three decades, he missed her. If he knew where she was, and begged, would she ever come back to him? Unlikely, she despised weakness in all its forms and she would see through him in an instant.

He sank into the dusty sofa and opened the paper wrapping of his dinner, allowing the warm and comforting smell of batter, grease, salt and vinegar to fill the air. That was another thing he had struggled to get used to. The need to eat, drink and sleep. It had soon become unnervingly apparent that in the mortal realm immortality was not the same as invulnerability. Many had refused to adapt to mortal needs, adamant that compromise was a weakness. They had been the first to fade, especially if their stories had passed from memory. Charon was not so easily beaten. He had been around since the first mortal had passed on, springing from the collective imagination of humanity, and appointed himself gatekeeper: a guardian of the dead. Why had he done nothing when Zeus and the others took over? The short answer was that he didn't want the job himself. Too much hassle. It was easier to just keep his head down, not draw attention to himself, and not make a fuss.

Charon sighed. He had been such a pushover then and now he didn't have the first idea how to broach the subject with Ra. Ra had no right to issue orders to him, but nor did he have any obligation to listen. *What's the worst he could do to me?* That was an easy one. Ra could throw him out of the building with a thought... via the window.

This was not a pleasant prospect, but he could not sit and do nothing, not again. It would not just be the gods who suffered from Ra's high-handedness but humans too. They had suffered already due to the games of the gods. Their egos and conflicts had repercussions which never seemed to touch them in the way it touched humans. While they had been expelled from their former home after Yahweh had won that stupid bet, and kicked them all out, it had not been the sole reason for their exile.

If a mortal was found worshipping a rival, or disparaging them, woe betide them. Hippolytus found that out the hard way when he got caught in that squabble between Artemis and Aphrodite, and his poor step-mother was used as a pawn in the process. *We deserve to fade away, but the mortals? They are stuck. They have one home and Ra plans to destroy it and them with it just so that he can go home. It cannot be allowed. Not this time*, he thought to himself.

As he passed through the kitchen on the way up to the bathroom he hurled the paper from his meal at the bin, not caring if it hit its target. Maybe he should talk to Odin? His name had been scrubbed off the list for a reason and it would be interesting to find out why. As he brushed his teeth he considered his options. Odin stood no more chance of being receptive than Ra did. One thing was certain: he dared not go via Hades or his brothers. That would give away his little indiscretion straight away and he would never find out anything. He wondered when he had become such a coward. 'I'm thinking like Hermes now.'

Talking to yourself again, old man. Never a good sign.

He glanced at his phone to check the time and noticed he had a message. Assuming it was spam as only Hades, and now Hermes, had his number he waited for his phone to wake up so he could delete it and block the number. 'Bloody spammers!' he muttered as he fumbled with the screen. Eventually his phone responded, and he held it at arm's length to focus properly on the screen. Nobody had warned him that his choice for a mature human form came with aches, pains, and failing eyesight. Trust the gods to come up with that one. Zeus probably thought it was funny, but he still looked no more than thirty. Finally, the message opened.

'Your involvement in this matter is neither required nor welcome. If you continue to interfere, your position will become very uncomfortable.'

Oh crap! How had he been found out? Looking for the sender's number he saw it was withheld. He thought that Hermes might be able to help him find out who sent it, but not right now. There was now a bigger question in the air. How did whoever sent this know what he knew, not to mention what he was considering?

He had only spoken to Hermes about this. *Had Hermes said something?* Charon shook himself. No. Hermes was his friend. In thousands of years, he had never given him any reason to distrust him. Even after losing touch for, what was it, a century plus some change? Hermes was solid, at least where he was concerned, and it was good to have his friend back. Why would he betray him? There was nothing to gain from that. One thing was for sure. Someone had said something to someone and whoever that someone was, they were not happy. Out of sheer pique over being told what to do, he decided that first thing tomorrow he was going to march into Ra's office and confront him over both his 'plan' and over that message.

CHAPTER 4

An Unwelcome Guest

The waiting room at Ra's office was not much better than the foyer where Charon worked. The carpets were serviceable, the walls appeared to have been recently painted, but the furniture was worn and threadbare. The room was empty of people bar the receptionist, an austere-looking woman who appeared to be in her late forties but looks could be deceiving when dealing with the Gods and their associates. Her desk was placed very deliberately between the entrance and the waiting room. She looked sternly at him over her horn-rimmed cats'-eye spectacles from which trailed a string of what looked like glass beads. He saw her take his measure and find him lacking.

'Good morning, Mr Charon.'

Well that's creepy, he thought. He had not made

an appointment, let alone met this woman before. Her voice had a slight Nubian lilt. Was she one of them? She clearly knew who he was which meant that he was at an immediate disadvantage. How had they known he was coming?

'I'm here to speak with your employer. No, I don't have an appointment, and before you ask, it's a confidential matter, so don't even bother,' Charon snapped. He generally had little time for receptionists.

'Well, we are in a bad mood this morning, aren't we? If you will take a seat, I will see if he can fit you in…'

'I'm not asking Miss…'

'Hathor. Since we have never met, I will forgive your disrespect. Once. I admire your directness, but please do not mistake me for a mere desk clerk again.' She was now, inexplicably, standing face to face with him, smiling, but it was not a friendly smile and it did not meet her eyes. It was more like a snarl. He tried to shake the foggy feeling that was settling over him. 'Take a seat, Mr Charon.' With that, she wove her way around the furniture toward the office.

His watch told him it was now quarter past one. 'Okay, but I don't have long. I have...' Then she was gone.

So, that was Hathor. On the scale of terrifying women, she had to be up there with Hera, but on the upside, at least she hadn't vaporised him. He looked up and she had gone. Had he heard the door close? He sighed as he realised that the room had deliberately been laid out to place obstacles between visitors and the office door. After using the vending machine to produce a tiny cup of a scalding hot, bitter, tar-like substance which claimed to be coffee, and dropping said cup in the bin, he selected a chair next to the table with the magazines. He flicked through the pile and found, to his disgust, that they were all about management consultancy and how to squeeze the most out of a workforce stopping only a fraction short of shackling people to desks, cracking whips or drawing blood. As far as Charon was concerned, the only people less productive than management consultants were restaurant critics, but at least they took you out for dinner before screwing you.

Next to the pile was a plastic holder for business

cards. It was nearly empty and at some point someone had attempted to tape over a crack. Like everything else in the room the tape had begun to turn yellow and curl up at the edges. *More decay*, thought Charon. 'We cling, and we cling, and around us everything crumbles.' He pocketed a card. *So much for marching in and having it out with him.*

He glanced at the clock. He then checked his watch. That was weird. Forty minutes had passed but he would have sworn that he had been waiting no longer than ten. What had happened to the time? Charon shivered. He was used to feeling that time passed quickly for him, but that was merely a matter of perception. Here it was actually passing more quickly. More importantly, he was going to be late for work and that would be noticed. Well, he was here now. He had thought about calling in sick but nobody would believe that. Doing so now would raise some uncomfortable questions. He hadn't booked a day off or taken a sick day in ten centuries.

'Mr Charon,' the velvety voice of Hathor broke the silence. 'Ra will see you now. You have ten minutes.'

'Thanks.' Charon made his way across the room

and had to slow down. The floor felt wrong. Insubstantial. The door was only a few meters from him but somehow it was both closer and further away at the same time. This was worse than being drunk and it made him feel sick. Hopefully, it would not be necessary to come here again. The door opened by itself and shut behind him. He glanced back in time to see Hathor back at her desk as if she had never left it.

Ra did not seem pleased to see him. 'Good morning, Mr Charon.' The office reflected the waiting room. The wallpaper was peeling under the tiny window near the ceiling above Ra's chair. 'I am given to understand you have something private to discuss with me. So great it seems was your need, that you appear to have forgotten to pay due respect to both me and to my assistant. Before we begin this discussion, let me make it clear that after today, you will not come here again.'

Suspicion confirmed. Here goes nothing, he thought. 'I can't let you do it.'

Ra said nothing. He leant forwards in his chair and rested his elbows on the desk. His golden eyes shone despite the lack of light in the room but gave away nothing of his mood. In earlier days, he could have swept Charon away with a thought. Unfortunately, Ra's vanity appeared to have survived his weakening powers, but the mark of human belief had left its mark on him. The bridge of his nose was just a little too high and wide to be wholly human and there was something very birdlike in his mannerisms. It made Charon's skin crawl, but he still tried to stare Ra down.

'Let me?' Ra laughed. 'Let me? You appear to be labouring under the assumption that you can stop me.' The laughter left his face as quickly as it had appeared, and his voice became hard.

No one who could switch moods that fast should be tangled with.

'Let *me* dispossess you of that idea now.' Ra gestured to a spot in front of his desk. While he had no power over Charon, obedience appeared to be the prudent choice, so he followed the instruction.

Ra was used to getting his own way, *but not this time*, Charon thought. 'You are talking about ending the world because you're bored. You've had enough so you're shutting up shop, turning out the lights and dragging the rest of us out along with you. Had it not occurred to you that some of us aren't ready to quit? You cannot just decide for us.'

'You go too far, Charon.' Ra's eyes flared again.

Back off, old man. Charon thought.

'Do not think I have not considered my actions. I advise you to remember your place.'

'Why now? You've lived around humans for centuries now. Why suddenly quit now?' He shifted his weight from one foot to the other and tried not to look away. That stare was really making him feel uneasy. *Two can play that game,* he thought, and Charon glowed back at him.

'Good! Now you are asking the right questions. It is never good to make assumptions. Sit.' Ra waved his perfectly manicured hand lazily at the end of the desk, and an ornate enamel-work tray appeared, holding a matching coffee pot and two matching cups. The smell was unmistakable.

'You'll find this far more palatable than the swill

from the machine. I only keep that there for appearance's sake. My powers are returning, but more slowly than I would like and they are not what they once were. I will need them at full-strength before I can carry out my plan. I also have other preparations to make.' He handed a cup to Charon. 'Forgive me, you have no chair.' He waved his hand and one of the scruffy chairs from the waiting room appeared behind him. 'I am sorry. Were you expecting something grander?' He had obviously seen Charon's expression. 'Sadly, I cannot yet make anything materialise which does not already exist in the mortal world. There is also a limit to the range to which my powers extend. Two or three rooms away appears to be the limit. As I said, it will take me time to regain my full strength. You still have a year.'

Charon took the cup, wondering when Ra would get to the point. He was dubious about eating or drinking anything served to him in this office, but he needed to appear cooperative. Offending Ra would not get him what he wanted. It was already likely to come with a penalty.

'Normal time? I spent what felt like ten minutes in the other room, yet my watch and your clock both leapt forwards by forty minutes.'

'Yes, that does rather disorient people the first time they come across it. I charge by the hour, so accelerating it is just one way of adding a few more minutes onto the invoices. What I do doesn't take very long – not the way I do it – so this little parlour trick simply adds oil to the gears. Besides which, the sort of human who employs my services wouldn't trust me if I charged less.' He smirked then. Actually smirked 'Too scared to lead but dying to be in charge. Literally.'

Oh, very clever smart boy. What else are you stealing from them? thought Charon. On second thought, he didn't want to know. Ra was evading his first question. He had reasons. *What reasons!?* He sipped his coffee and considered another angle to approach the issue from while Ra continued to drone on about himself and how brilliant he thought himself to be. Charon was now certain that Ra's plan came, not from any malice, but from total self-interest. He simply didn't care about anyone but himself. The man could have taught Narcissus a thing or two. He'd been another total waste of space, if you asked Charon. He'd had to practically drag Narcissus away from the edge of the Styx, when he realised there were no mirrors in the Underworld. *Stupid boy.*

'Yes, thanks for the sales-pitch and everything, but you still haven't told me why you suddenly intend to end the world just so you can take an extra-long bath with your bestie? Some of us have to get back to work, so I'd appreciate it if you got to the bloody point.'

'You came for 'answers', Mr Charon, but you are mistaken if you thought they would be free. I have not asked you how you know what I said in that meeting because I already know.'

'Yes, and you, or one of your flunkies, sent me a text warning me off. If I remember the 'rules', your lot can't tell me what to do…'

'I am sorry to disappoint you, but I know nothing of any messages, and while it is true that I cannot give you orders, I *can* issue an official complaint to your own superiors about your interference, which I will do if you continue to press this issue.' Ra poured himself another coffee. His eyes were flaring again.

Probably best to ease off a bit now, Charon's

better judgement warned him as the reprimand continued. He cleared his throat and put his cup down gently.

Ra continued, 'For now, I shall say nothing but I will remind you that you came here unannounced and uninvited, demanding that I give you my time at no charge. Your courage has impressed me *this once*.' That had all sorts of connotations attached to it. Charon swallowed. 'I have allowed you this meeting for one reason: my own amusement and when I am no longer entertained the meeting will end, not before. Now, ask your questions.' Ra's voice was cold and hard, and Charon needed no persuasion that he meant every word.

'How do you plan to regain your powers? You can't possibly think we still have any influence here, Ra. The mortals are forgetting us as we speak.'

'How I plan to do this is not your concern. Let's just say that my plans have borne fruit and are progressing nicely. Next question.'

'Back to my first question. Why?'

'You think I am the worst thing that can happen to

you? No. Unlike your own superiors, I keep track of those I am responsible for and my connections among the lower deities have been bringing me disturbing reports for months. There is a danger coming that, in our diminished physical forms, none of us can hope to defend against. I decided to act. That is all.'

'What danger? Did it not occur to you to share this information with the rest of us?'

'Share? Why should I share? Where were the rest of you when that manipulative, petty, pretender Yahweh, spread his influence across our lands, forcing us to take physical form just to survive?'

'They hardly...'

'They. Let. It. Happen! That bet, to use a human idiom, was just the icing on the cake. They were all far too busy squabbling and picking fights with each other to even notice. When they did pay attention, it was only to play with the head of some poor mortal who had done nothing more than worship the wrong god. Or do something petty to another woman because her husband couldn't keep his toga down around mortals. Yes, we got the news about Hera's little acts of revenge. The whole immortal realm could hear that woman on one of her rants! Sometimes I almost felt sorry for Zeus but then your friends made that stupid drunken bet, knowing that he would cheat, and suddenly we're all out. Tell me. How does what I plan differ from the terms of that bet? It wasn't just Dionysus who got thrown out, it was all of us! Over a cosmic bloody pissing-contest!'

'Fine, I'll give you that one'. Hera had an extremely nasty streak, but it occurred to him that Ra and the rest of the Egyptians were just as guilty of 'squabbling' among themselves. Now was probably not a good time to point that out though. He also had to agree with him on the sharing front. None of them was great at volunteering information which might give a rival any assistance. The 'problem shared' mantra was not their style. Losing the bet? The gods had been losing influence long before then and, through that, their powers. Getting them to admit that was another matter.

They had assumed they would always have influence. To many, their very existence had confirmed it, but the gods had been neglectful and cruel. Those who had retained influence were still too strong, and Yahweh had not had the power to throw all of them out, but those who had been expelled had always mistaken fear for respect and had lost their genuine support long before then. Something kept them present and whole in the mortal realm. It wasn't until popular memory of them began to fade, and them with it, that they realised how much they really had relied on mortal belief. As more stories began to fade out of human consciousness, more of them simply disappeared. Hesiod and Homer were, well, a godsend. Thanks to them, they had been able to maintain a hold on their existence, however tenuous. Even though they had lost their followers, they still had tangible ties to this world.

'So you're sulking?' Charon asked.

'No.'

'Yes. You are.' Charon stood up and leant over the desk, almost nose to nose with Ra. His better judgment jumped up and down in his head, screaming at him to for gods' sake, shut up and sit down. He ignored it. 'You've just told me that you're giving up without a fight because you don't want to ask for help fighting something which none of us will be able to fight alone. Never mind that your solution means we all go with you.' He paused. 'But that's not the whole story is it? Your 'solution', as you put it, means saving your own selfish carcass. You never had any intention of taking any of us back with you.' He felt something in him shift then, as if letting some long-buried aspect of another incarnation out of the shadows. His already pale skin began to glow along with his eyes. This was rage, and it felt good to finally let it out. He felt like his old self again, but no, this was better. The centuries of merging stories had imbued him with the power of Death. Not the same being, but all the same, he could do with every advantage and he was certain that Ra had not seen this coming, 'And you have actually told people about your plan because you cannot resist gloating. It's not enough for you to know you have won, you need to drive that point home too. As half-baked, maniacal plan's go, yours is up there with Lex Luthor's!'

'Who?'

'Popular culture. I would have thought that considering what is keeping us all here, you might have paid a bit more attention.'

'Oh, that. Well, only insofar as it serves my purpose. I keep throwing money at the arts but they plough straight through it. Those humans do love to dig things up though. I simply make a profitable strategic location known every decade or so, and presto, we are suddenly 'alive' in public consciousness again.'

'You manipulative bastard!'

Ra feigned a pout, 'I don't see Zeus or anyone doing anything to keep us from fading away. Besides which, I would never be so crude as to resort to direct manipulation. Unlike that usurping whelp. Who do you think put the idea to convert into Constantine's head in the first place? The battle of Milvian Bridge[iv]? Yahweh set Dionysus up for a fall by raising the stakes like that and you were all too busy griping and backbiting to see it. He'd had one of his flunkies whispering in Constantine's ear for months before that battle. To be thrown out of *my* realm by a mere boy was humiliating enough. Imagine my disquiet when I discovered why?' Charon swore he could hear Ra's teeth grind.

Dionysus had already been punished for his part

in the bet. He was still under supervision of the Council and had been expressly forbidden from gambling in any form. He wasn't even allowed to buy a lottery ticket. If Ra ever got back to the immortal realm, there was going to be one hell of a punch-up and there were some very angry immortals down here just lining up to take a swing at him. 'I have had enough of explaining myself to you. It is decided and there is nothing you or anyone else can do to stop me.' Ra smirked again.

Charon's anger at Ra's arrogance was giving him heartburn but at least he had some answers. Ra's scheme was total self-preservation. He wasn't even particularly keen to go back, he just didn't want to be beaten by... whatever it was that was coming. The self-satisfied git was just looking after number one. 'Are you going to at least tell me what this big threat to our existence is?'

'No.'

'Just 'no'?'

'As far as I am concerned, Mr Charon, the matter is closed. I have made my decision and my plans are in motion. I cannot allow you to disrupt them and your opinion on the matter is not required. You may now leave my office.'

The office door was suddenly open. Charon knew it would be very dangerous to stay any longer and he doubted he would get more out of Ra anyway. He decided he would put in a last favourite parlour trick of his own. As he closed the door behind him he lowered the temperature in the office to the point that Ra could see his breath, and no amount of artificial heat could fix it. He promptly left the building before he was hauled back in to put it right.

CHAPTER 5

A friend in deed?

He waited until he had got around the corner before calling Hermes. It was already getting dark, but he could have been in Ra's office for no more than an hour. Somehow a whole day had passed. He checked the time by looking through the window of a nearby car. It was an old model and so still had an analogue dashboard clock. Quarter to five. Damn Ra and his stupid time tricks. He must be getting stronger already. Charon knew that his absence from his post would have been noted now despite his efforts. No point going back now. The caretakers would lock up and the night-watch would be in soon. His hands shook a little as he pulled out his phone.

'Hello?' Hermes answered within a few rings.

'Pub. Fifteen minutes.'

'Charon? Is that you?' *Stupid question...* Charon didn't bother to listen to the rest and didn't want to discuss it down the phone so hung up.

* * *

Charon sat at the same table as before, but this time he was facing the bar. He didn't like the attitude of the barman who had resumed his pastime of giving him funny looks. As Charon calmed down he lost some of the glow from his skin and what hadn't faded was hidden under his hood, but even so, the boy had no manners. Hermes arrived and ordered himself a drink before joining him. He hadn't even sat down before Charon spoke.

'I went to see Ra. To get to the bottom of why the hell he thinks that he can take us all with him.'

'You did what! How the hell did you get out?'

'Wasn't hard. He practically threw me out.' Charon laughed. 'He wasn't at all pleased to see me. Said I was to mind my own business, keep my mouth shut, and that I was never to turn up there again.' He decided it was probably best not to tell him about his little trick with the thermostat. It wouldn't impress Hermes, but it still made him smile. *Small victories always make life worth living.*

'What in Hel's name possessed you to go there?'

'This.' He showed Hermes the text message that came through last night. 'Did you tell anyone what I said yesterday?'

'Who would I tell? I'm not stupid enough to broadcast that. If they thought for a moment that I had anything to do with it, they would roast me alive. Lord knows what they would do if they actually found me interfering.'

'Still scared of Daddy?' Charon teased. It wasn't fair really. Hermes had basically been the boot boy for the lot of them. Errands, diversions, subterfuge. Now he had a modicum of extra freedom from them, Charon couldn't blame him for not wanting to risk it.

'Terrified, and you would be too if you had any sense. I don't want your newly emerging heroic streak coming back to bite me. Remember, I don't exactly have a spotless reputation.'

'The dice thing?'

'And the rest!' Hermes dropped his voice. 'I hacked into my personnel file. *'Opportunistic trouble maker, not to be trusted as far as you can kick him,'* he recited in a nasal sing-song voice. 'In short, I am probably, if not certainly, being watched. If they catch me anywhere near this, I am a dead man.' Charon felt his ire rising again. This wasn't the Hermes that he knew. He'd had enough of the defeatism. 'Charon, mate, I know this has gotten to you, but we don't have any idea what the others are planning. I can't see Zeus or Hades sitting back and taking this quietly and they have a terrible track record when it comes to shooting the messenger.'

'Taking what? Herm, we have no idea what we are up against and they still think this is just another one of Ra's tantrums. We haven't heard a word from any of them.'

'It's only been a day.'

'There is that.' Charon paused. 'All Ra said was

that his plan was a solution to a bigger problem. One we can't fight. He's just given up, but it's worse than that.'

'How can it possibly get worse than the end of the world?'

'Two ways. Firstly, I don't entirely believe him. Secondly, even if he can be 'trusted' he has decided for all of us that we can't beat whatever is coming and taken it upon himself to embark on a solution that means only he gets to survive while the rest of us are left to face it. By refusing to tell us, he is making sure he comes out on top. If we knew what it was we could at least work together to stop it but he's not spilling.'

'Yeah, I can see that happening,' Hermes said, fiddling with the coaster absently, 'Did you ever leave the 1960s, mate?'

'It was a good decade.' Charon grinned and downed half of his pint. Gods, he felt tired. That trick with the temperature had left him drained. It had been foolish to show off like that. Especially as he had probably really annoyed Ra. *He won't forget that in a hurry and he is actively trying to rebuild his power.* The temperature in there should return to normal in a couple of days. Even so, Charon was not looking forward to coming face to face with him again. 'I need your help, Hermes. You are closer to the top than I am. I'm sure you can keep your ears open, do some digging, find out what the hell is going on.'

'I told you already, I am not fishing around!' Hermes leaned back in his chair and folded his arms. 'Look. I do understand and if I hear something I will let you know, but I am not going looking for it. That is suicide. I might be able to trace that message though. Lend me your phone.' Charon hesitated, 'I'm not going to eat it. Relax. You'll get it back tomorrow.'

Charon considered this for a moment. Hermes was probably right to want to stay out of it, but Charon felt he was in too deep now and he was not ready to just give up and wait for the end to hit him in the face. He needed to know what *'It'* was. 'Very well.' Charon passed it over. 'I'll meet you back here at the same time tomorrow so you can return it. Thanks, Herm.'

'Don't thank me yet. I haven't made any promises

and I still think you are being a pig-headed old fool. You've been warned off. Twice! Yet here you go off on a mission that you are not equipped to take on. Didn't thousands of years on that river teach you to leave the heroics to the heroes?' Hermes was getting over excited now and the coaster had been reduced to confetti.

'Sshhh! Keep your voice down!' Charon hissed at him.

Hermes ignored him, 'Since you are determined to take stupid risks, I *will* keep an ear open. Just don't go doing that sort of damned foolish thing again.'

'Going soft in your old age?'

'Not even close, old man!' Hermes laughed and downed the last of his pint. 'Come on, I'm hungry and all they serve here are snacks.'

As they left the pub, the green haired barman glared at their backs then watched them through the window. After they had rounded the boundary hedge, he pulled out his phone and hit the speed-dial simply named 'C'.

A. H. Johnstone

CHAPTER 6

The Fae are Displeased

The following morning went about as well as Charon expected. He slept through his alarm, tripped over the stupid cat, spilled hot coffee down his only clean shirt and missed his bus. It was still dark when he left the house, and drizzling, so he walked, cold and soaked as waiting for the next bus would have made him later. It wouldn't do to draw any more attention.

He had considered using some of his power to shield himself from the rain, but he couldn't afford to squander it on his personal comfort. He might need it later. Who knew if he would be able to regain it? There had been no sign yet that the power he had could replenish in the mortal world so he dared not indulge. Showing off yesterday had been a mistake, and he regretted it. It's just that Ra was so insufferably smug! *No matter. I should not have provoked him. He's probably watching me already.*

He thought back to the text message that Ra claimed had been nothing to do with him. Had Hermes traced it yet? He was due to meet him later to get his phone back but this did nothing to ease his anxiety and was no help at all when it came to deciding what to do next. The feeling that he was being watched was deeply uncomfortable, but it wasn't like he was unused to being supervised.

Unlocking the side door to let himself in, he noticed that the night watch had left their usual carnage behind them. Empty takeaway wrappers and unwashed crockery were strewn over the little table in the kitchen. Their absence meant he was late. *Oh, well*, he thought. *What are they going to do? Sack me? I should be so bleeding lucky.*

The light flickered and he sighed. *Something else to fix.* His mood was not improved by the incessant buzzing. Minor annoyances were snow-balling into a grinding resentment, and suspicion that the last nineteen centuries' niggling irritations had been a personal campaign against him which culminated in this bloody stupid power game. He knew they hadn't been. Not really. His superiors simply didn't care enough to bother. He was just a useful tool. A gatekeeper to a building. They hadn't even bothered to tell him why an empty building needed to be guarded at all times. Thanatos had never toyed with him like this. He had just let him get on with his job. The Furies and the Fates on the other hand? They were a different matter.

He shuddered and tried again to remember what Ra had promised to Osiris. It was no good. Even immortal memory wasn't perfect and the longer he lived the more he had to try to make space for. At first the fine details would fade until eventually he'd lost whole chunks of his existence. Diaries didn't help either. After a while some things were just so far removed that it was like reading about someone else's life. Not that he was complaining: his life before coming to the mortal world had been unbelievably boring. Secretly, the real reason he kept 'accidentally' letting mortals cross the Styx was to break the monotony, not to mention the sheer satisfaction of seeing their faces on the other side. Dante had been livid, *'the presumptuous berk'*. He wished his memory loss could be a bit more selective. His thoughts wandered to Hel. Had she forgotten him? He wouldn't blame her. She'd hated the facade of a mortal life and had not been shy about expressing herself. Then, one day, she was just gone.

The kettle came to the boil and dragged him out of his thoughts. He didn't have time to feel sorry for himself. He had to move on and now even this bleak existence was at stake. The door to the foyer was ajar but open far enough that he could catch a glimpse of something out of the corner of his eye. He should have been the only one there. He placed the cup down as silently as he could and moved toward the door. Peering through the gap between the hinge and the frame he could make out a portion of the desk and, over the top, the upper portion of the front doors. Nothing moved for what seemed an eternity.

Again, something flashed past the door, only inches from his nose, and he jerked his head back in shock. Whatever it was, was too fast for him to focus clearly on. He peered out again. Was it aware of his presence? Did he want it to be? This was probably Ra messing with him in return for yesterday, but what creature of his could move like that? Charon hadn't really mixed outside the various groups of demons and deities from the Underworld, so who knew what Ra had in his tool kit?

Something was out there, there was no doubt about it. He could hear it whistling around the foyer. His foyer! Enough of this nonsense! He was going out there to send whatever it was on its way and out of his. Just as soon as he could convince his legs that it was a good idea. They were, as yet, not budging on the matter. How long had he been there now? Two minutes? Five? He had to do something but what? Maybe he should find out what it wanted first. 'Fine.' he said aloud and marched out to his desk. Had it been frightened off? The cavernous room appeared empty after a cursory glance but on closer examination he could hear giggling coming, very faintly, from a cobweb covered plastic fern in the opposite corner.

'Whoever you are, you have five seconds to stop messing me around and get out here before I call the police!'

The leaves rustled once more and whatever it was shot out and started buzzing around his head. The 'it' turned out to be three tiny winged children. This was not good. They might appear to be children but they could well be older than he was and, more importantly, more powerful. Charon knew better than to judge by appearances. If they were what he suspected them to be then they were to be neither trusted nor tangled with. The stories of what happened to mortals caught meddling in Faery affairs were not an exaggeration. He was not mortal but this was no time to pick hairs.

'Can I help you?' It grated at every nerve he had to have to be so deferent to what he regarded as pests, but it was unwise to offend them.

'It is we who can help you,' they said in unison. He felt the voices rather than heard them. 'We come with a final warning, Ferryman. Your current path is unsafe. Walk away. Your involvement is not required.'

'Who sent you?' Charon frowned. The last two days had been weird. He mentally corrected that to 'weirder than normal'. Generally, mortals didn't bother manning the front desks of buildings they had long-since abandoned. However, that wasn't to stop his superiors. They wanted to put on a good show but it would have helped if any of them had bothered to read the script. *Leave it to the understudies.*

'We can say no more than it comes from the Fae. We were given a message to pass on to you and, if asked, to tell you that your attempts to trace your previous warning will fail. You interfere in matters which do not concern you.' The creature's voice was flat. They gave no hint of emotion but that was no bad thing. Learning that the Fae were displeased was very often a terminal experience.

He decided to fob them off and get rid of them. 'I don't know what you are talking about--'

Before the words had passed his lips, the creatures transformed themselves into human adult form, surrounded by blue, silver and green flames swirling around them. The blast of power which exploded from the transformation knocked Charon backwards onto the floor and he landed hard. Pain surged up his back and down his leg and, momentarily, he could only lie there and wait for it to ease enough to get up.

'Do not lie to us and do not think us foolish!' The

silver one snapped. 'You have already interfered!' It moved closer and leaned over him. The amiable cherubic face of the child had vanished under chiselled features of what appeared to be a young man in his mid to late twenties. Only this one was blue. Charon was now close enough to the creature to feel the draught under his enormous wings but he dared not offend it further by looking it in the eye. *Damn it,* he thought, *I should have known better than that.* The creature's dark blue hair appeared to bristle, as it bent lower, with rage and indignation after being so blatantly lied to. Charon then realised that it had not hair but feathers. Was this a glamour? Very few had seen the true appearance of one of the Fae and survived to tell the tale. What came next took Charon by surprise. The creature sighed and folded its arms. 'Why do you cower? You are no mere mortal, and we are not here to harm you! Get up!'

'I apologise for the insult. I did not wish to offend you further. Please, allow me a few moments. I fell hard, and I am not as young as I look.'

'Nor am I. The intent is appreciated, but unnecessary. The warning is for your own protection.

You do not have the power to do anything about what is coming.'

'I can't just do nothing,' Charon snapped as he groaned and struggled to his feet, then limped back to his chair. He sat slowly, wincing, as the seat took his weight. 'I found out enough yesterday to tell me that much. If Ra is permitted to carry out his plan, we all die. He's the only one who'll get out of this alive.'

'Ra?' He signalled the other two who began examining him.

'Yes, Ra! Tall fella. Gold eyes. Smug. Thinks he can push everyone around, including me. Ow! Stop prodding will you?'

'My friends only wish to ease your pain. It was not our intention to cause injury. We were not expecting to find an old man.' The creatures had thankfully ceased their light show. Unfortunately, the now absent flames had concealed the fact they were completely naked. He didn't know where to look but suggesting they don mortal clothes might well provoke them again. He would just have to focus above the waist.

'Yes, well, this was the body I got, and I don't have the luxury of swapping for a shiny new one whenever the fancy takes me. Before you ask, no I don't want you to do anything. I know better than that. Faery magic always comes with a catch.'

'Very well,' he smiled. 'You were saying?'

'What? Oh. Yes. Ra. He says he has heard that something big and scary is on its way, only he's decided to keep exactly what that is to himself. He's come up with some big idea to survive and won't say what it is or when it's due in case someone tries to stop him.'

'This is something we should report back to our employer.' He frowned.

'Since when did fairies have employers? I thought you lot were above all that?'

'Yes. Generally we are, but we have an arrangement.'

'Dare I ask who with? No. Forget it. I don't want to know.' Charon pinched the bridge of his nose. 'Look, lads, I really appreciate the sentiment. I have a mysterious benefactor somewhere that doesn't want me to get hurt. That's just great.' He wondered if the Fae understood sarcasm. 'But the creepy warnings can stop. Now. I don't have time for all that and I am old enough to look after myself.'

'You are not equipped for what is to come. It is unwise for you to pursue this. It will not end well if you do.'

'Oh, and what exactly is to come? Look, nobody but me seems at all bothered about what happened in that meeting so unless I do something about it, equipped or otherwise, it looks like the rest of us get to play bit parts and get caught in it anyway. If I hadn't been caught eavesdropping…'

'You were not caught eavesdropping. You were overheard talking about it. Loudly. In a very public place. You lack discretion, Charon, and you risk exposing us all. It is a good thing it was our man who heard you, not someone else. It has taken us great trouble to convince the mortals that we are not real, and we would like it to stay that way. Other than that, we would rather not get involved with the petty squabbles of fallen gods. You are here at our discretion and that means there are rules! If mortals get wind that we aren't as imaginary as we have made ourselves out to be, we will be in great peril. Their prejudice and fear has not decreased for all that their technology has advanced. We are not ignorant of their ways and know precisely what the more curious would do to one of us if we were caught.'

He could well understand this fear but, for now, Charon had heard enough, 'If I can't stop Ra, along with whatever has him so spooked he thinks that ending the world is the only way to stop the world ending with him in it, we're all dead. You, me, the mortals, everyone. Your cover being blown will be the least of our problems.' The expressions on their faces were enough to tell him that this idea had taken them by surprise, but they were not arguing with him. *So, faeries aren't quite so all knowing after all*. 'I have a message for you to take back: thanks, but *no thanks*. If I am the only one who has any intention of trying to fight this, that's just how it must be. I might fail but at least I will have tried. What can the rest of you say? Hmm? Would you really rather be swallowed by the sea because you're scared of blowing your cover, or too proud to work with fallen gods? Fine. You lot do what suits you, but don't get in my way!'

'Very well. We will pass on your message but we cannot protect you if you ignore this warning. We know a little about what is going on and might be what your friend, Ra, is afraid of.'

'He's not my friend.'

'Irrelevant.' He sighed. The relations between other races were of no interest to him. He cocked one dark blue eyebrow and looked at Charon with what could best be described as contempt. His tone had become flat and impassive again, 'If you come to the old paint factory at midnight tonight there will be a meeting. If you are careful you may be able to observe them. I do not know what it concerns, just that some highly influential figures will be present. If you decide to go, you must go alone. We cannot protect you if you defy us.' With that, they all transformed themselves back into the tiny creatures which had first greeted him and disappeared through the broken ceiling window.

It took Charon a moment to compose himself. Faery magic was known to leave mortals feeling foggy but for it to have worked on him was just embarrassing. He knew one thing. He did not want their help and he made a mental note to visit a farrier for some iron nails to hide around the threshold. Modern steel didn't quite work as well for some reason. He needed to take this in. It was getting weird. Someone was definitely watching him then, but at least it seemed to be benevolent. It irked him that they seemed to know what he was going to do even before he did. All they cared about was their own cover. *They say mortals are selfish and greedy but have we really been the best examples?* What was he talking about? The gods had gained more than their power from their stories. Their nature, or at least part of it, came from what was believed about them and, while the gods had revelled in their stories as a form of worship, they became inseparably linked to them. All the jealousy, greed, fear, distrust and vengeance of an immature species had been rolled up and packed into a divine shell.

He pulled out Hermes's phone and rang his own. It rang several times before he answered. 'Any luck?'

A muffled 'No. Why? What's happened? More messages?' came back to him. He silently wished

Hermes would not try to eat and talk on the phone.

'You could say that. What do you know about faeries?'

There was a crash of a desk chair hitting lino in the background. He waited for him to pick up the phone again. 'Hello? Still there? Charon, I know enough to stay well away from them. Whatever they have offered you, say 'no'.' Hermes did not sound amused.

'Relax. They warned me off. That's all. We were heard talking and someone in that pub reported back to them. I wasn't caught eavesdropping.' Charon told Hermes about his encounter with his unlikely 'allies'. As he recounted it, he considered that it was a good thing that Hermes was like him, because what he was saying sounded totally mad. Even the most spaced out hippie in the world would have been giving him funny looks and edging away.

'Okay. Charon, I know the last couple of days have been weird, but are you feeling okay? Faeries are not exactly known for their generosity. More for being tricky, devious, callous, mean-spirited little bastards. I wouldn't trust them if my life depended on it.'

'You could sound pleased?'

'Why? In what possible scenario could you imagine that I would be pleased about faeries showing up!?'

'Keep your voice down! I wasn't very happy about it either, but we now know whoever it was that sent that text is a friend. The Fae didn't know about Ra's plan so whatever Ra is running from probably doesn't know he knows either. Anyway, they told me to go to the old paint factory alone at midnight. You don't have to come in, but I could do with a lift.'

'You're winding me up, right?' Hermes spluttered. It sounded like he was choking on the other end of the line.

'Nope. If you're not up for it, I'll just call a taxi...'

'No way! I'm not letting you go wandering around up there alone. I'm in, if only to make sure you come back in one piece.'

'Oh, come on. What's the worst that could happen?'

CHAPTER 7

Subterfuge and Stealth... Sort Of

Hermes sounded the car horn outside Charon's house. As if in answer the lights began going out. Moments later Charon emerged from the house carrying torches and flasks under one arm, what looked like a cat under the other - it was not easy to tell exactly what lay under the spitting mass of ginger fur and bottle brush tail – with a key in his teeth. To Hermes he resembled a retired buccaneer. He sincerely hoped that Charon did not plan to get involved any further than he already was. Immortality was not the same as invulnerability, but Charon seemed to have forgotten that fact. They could still be hurt, and while it was rare, becoming ill was not unheard of. A yowl and a hiss, and the rattle of scattering beer cans told him that the 'cat' had had enough of being carried around like a large hairy rugby ball and had made an escape. Hermes watched as Charon limped across the road and got in the car.

'Stealthily done. I'm not sure if the whole street heard that. You should try to be louder next time.' He paused. 'What happened to you?' He asked as Charon buckled up. It amused him that the former ferryman of the dead was concerned about personal safety in a car while on the way to spy on a meeting between gods knew what. It also occurred to him that as said ferryman, Charon could well imagine every nasty scenario which could possibly take place. He stopped smirking and fastened his own.

'I upset a faerie.'

'You didn't tell me that the little bleeders beat you up!'

'Relax. It was an accident. Not that I am keen to repeat the experience, so if you must stay, for pity's sake, stay out of sight.'

'Which Pity? What has she got to do with it...' Hermes stammered.

'Not the one from the jar. Last I heard, Pandora

had managed to catch that one around about 2010.'

'Really? Hmm. I wondered where that one had got to....'

'Westminster,' said Charon. 'Let's get a shift on shall we? We still have a fifteen-minute drive and it's already twenty to midnight.'

'We don't want to risk being seen. We discussed this,' said Hermes, grinding the gears as he turned the car around.

'What happened to stealth and precision?'

'She's old okay?' Hermes drove in silence for several minutes. 'How come you never learned to drive?

'Hmm?' Charon said absently as he sipped from his flask.

'Driving?'

'Cars and I don't get along. They seem to just die, rather than be driven by me. I got through six of them before I worked that one out.'

This shut Hermes up. He hoped that whatever it was about his friend that made cars suicidal did not rub off on Suzie. At least until they were home in one piece. Finally, they arrived and he pulled up alongside the bramble-covered gates. There were no other cars there but this did not mean they were alone. He peered out of the window. It was so dark he could barely see the outline of the building. 'Are you sure this is a good idea?'

'I'm pretty sure it's not one of my better ones but we are here now. You know the plan?'

Hermes just stared.

'Fine. Let's go over it again. You take this.' He handed Hermes a torch. 'Then you climb up there.' He pointed to the ridged roof of the first building. It was low but would offer some cover. 'As soon as you are up there, turn off your torch. That way I will know the way is clear for me to find the meeting. Got it so far?'

Hermes continued to stare but this time he managed a nod.

Charon took this as his cue to continue, 'When I

find the meeting, I will start recording on my phone and streaming the video straight to yours like you showed me, so make sure it is on and on silent.'

This idea had impressed Hermes. Given Charon's intense dislike for all things technology, he had not expected him to come up with recording the meeting, let alone streaming it. He had said that if he were to be caught, he didn't want to be caught with the video on him. Either Charon was enjoying this, or he had been watching too many spy films. He suspected it was a bit of both.

'Hermes? Hermes? You got it?'

Hermes nodded.

'Good! Off you go. Good luck,' he said, cheerily.

Hermes got out of the car and closed the door as quietly as he could. The gate was rusty and squeaked as he squeezed his way through the gap. It did not look like it had been forced which meant they could be being watched. It was freezing which made it exceptionally hard to climb. He hoped that it wouldn't take too much longer to get to the top as the flask of hot soup he was carrying on a strap across his body swung and clanged against the old metal drainpipe he was scaling. Finally, he reached the top and hauled himself up over the edge. 'I must be a bloody idiot to get tangled up in this.' He muttered to himself.

'Not far off!' said a gruff voice in the dark and then something heavy met the back of Hermes' head.

* * *

Charon watched from the car as the torch went out. 'Nice one, Hermes!' He left the keys in the ignition, in case they needed to bid a hasty retreat, and made his way through the gate. As he picked his way through the rubbish and abandoned shopping trollies, it occurred to him that he should probably have told someone other than Hermes about where he was, but who would he tell? Even that hell beast of a cat wouldn't miss him until it got hungry. This is not an exaggeration. The 'cat' was an actual hellbeast that Charon had adopted for company before his move to the mortal realm. It was *not* friendly. He looked at his watch. It was three minutes past twelve. 'Damn! I'm missing it!'

A voice rang out of the silence, 'Oi! You there! Stop where you are!'

Charon felt his heart lurch in his chest and fell against a wall. 'What? Who's that?'

'It doesn't matter who we are. The faeries were right though.'

'What? That I wouldn't give up?' Charon struggled to speak as the fall had winded him. His chest ached terribly.

'No. They told us that the surest way to get you to do what we wanted you to do would probably be to tell you to do the opposite. You have spent too long around mortals, Charon. It has made you a foolish and stubborn old man,' said the voice.

The disembodied voice had not yet presented its owner to him so Charon stayed where he was. He had dropped his torch but it was still shining so its landing must have been cushioned. He slid down the wall to sit. Standing made him feel sick and dizzy and his heart was still pounding. He was excited but not to this extent. Something was wrong. Meeting be damned, he needed Hermes to get him out of there. Where was he?

A floodlight some way above him on the opposite wall clunked on and shone in his face as he leaned against the wall gasping for breath. He raised an arm to shield his eyes. *Oh crap, now I'm for it*. Running feet approached his position but he couldn't move. He reached into the inside of his jacket and pulled out a bottle of Gaviscon tablets and put two in his mouth. He wasn't quite sure what they would achieve at this point but maybe concentrating on the ghastly tablets slowly dissolving would help him stay calm. What did he have to lose?

'Good evening gents,' said Charon. There was a snarl in the background, 'ladies too, I see. Apologies. It appears my evening constitutional has intruded upon something I ought to stay out of. Might I intrude on your hospitality for a while longer and ask for one of you to call for an ambulance?'

One of the figures approached him. It was huge

but all Charon could make out was the silhouette. He couldn't focus. 'No ambulance will be needed. You will live. You only tripped one of our guard spells. Just as well you are not fully human, or we would not be having this conversation.' He sniffed. The voice was not familiar, but the accent was thick and Nordic. Was Hel there with her people? Had she sent them for him? He stopped himself. That longship had long ago sailed but the hope remained. No, this was not the work of Hel. She would never send mere men to deal with her loose ends. 'You'll come with us.' He whistled loudly and two others joined him. 'Take him to the van,' he paused. 'And do it carefully. We don't need a repeat of last time.' *What in the name of many Hells had happened the last time?*

'What? Where are you taking us…me? I won't go!'

'You will do as you are told, ferryman.' He turned to the people behind him. 'Bring his companion here. He'll stay with us. If Charon makes any attempt to escape, call me.'

Charon's heart began to pound again as two of them dragged Hermes forwards, one on each arm, into the light. His head lolled forwards and a trickle of blood ran down his neck but he couldn't see where it came from. From this angle, he could only see that his friend was unconscious and bleeding, and at the mercy of what he now assumed to be some of the less friendly former inhabitants of Asgard and Valhalla.

'What if I still refuse to go?' He wasn't sure what he expected to hear.

'We will deprive him of his head.'

'You can't! There are rules!' Charon rasped.

This was apparently the limit of his patience. 'Rules?' he roared. Whether out of rage or amusement, he couldn't tell. Then he marched up to Charon, grabbed him by the front of his jacket and hauled him to his feet and then off them again until they were nose to nose. 'You invade our territory and come to spy on us, and you talk to me of 'rules'?' The man's breath was hot on Charon's face, and he smelled of wood smoke.

'I... I didn't come to spy on you specifically...'

'Well, that's honourable. If this did not go above

my head old man, I would see that you did not leave with yours.' He dropped Charon back on his feet, planted a massive hand on his shoulder, and pressed his forehead against Charon's. His voice was so quiet it was barely audible. 'You will go with my men. You will go now, and you will go willingly. Once I get word that you have been delivered, I will release your friend and see that a healer attends him. Any trouble, I *will* kill him. I see no need to discuss this further.' He waved the men dragging Hermes away and nodded at two more to take Charon to the mystery van, then disappeared into the silhouetted crowd. As it closed around him, he felt their mailed gloves grab his arms and pull him in the same direction.

A. H. Johnstone

CHAPTER 8

Bad News of Titanic Proportions

From the feel of it, the walls of the van were soundproofed and solid, but they had put a bag over his head nonetheless. Charon sat gripping the edge of a bench and fought back waves of nausea as the van swerved around corners. He thought about pulling the bag off his head but that meant letting go of the bench and he was not sure if that was a good idea. He was beginning to feel more like himself, but the effects of the wards had drastically weakened him. He tried to take his mind off it but all he could think of was what they had done to Hermes. It took a great deal of force to render a god unconscious like that, and a human would not have been able to do it alone. Hermes would heal given time. Charon just hoped he would get out of this so that he could see to it that he got that time. Why had he brought him along? He had been told to come alone. 'Dammit!' he shouted at the air and punched the side of the van.

As if on cue, he heard a panel above his head slide open. 'Be quiet!'

'Where are you taking me?'

'To someone who wants to have a little word with you.' He turned to the driver and spoke in a language Charon didn't recognise. Whatever it was he said had clearly amused the driver who roared with laughter and swerved around another corner. Charon's stomach lurched as he fought back another wave. For all he knew, they had spent the last half an hour going around the block in a bid to disorientate him. If they were then it was working. The van suddenly slammed to a halt which sent Charon sprawling onto the floor. *'Enough!'* He ripped the bag from his head and clambered back to his feet as the doors opened.

They were at yet another abandoned factory. Lights were flickering behind the broken panes of glass from which he could hear singing and raucous laughter. Clearly, the party was in full swing. His escorts said nothing as they hauled him out of the van and up to the front doors. One of them attempted to force the bag back over Charon's head as they approached the building.

'Do you really think that is necessary?'

'We have our orders. You were not supposed to see the outside of this place. Hold still.'

'No. Look I have seen the place now. Besides, I like to see who is addressing me.' No sooner had he said this, then the door opened. Behind it stood what Charon at first glance assumed to be a bear. He was glaring at the man with the bag, but the shadow this figure cast over the three of them couldn't help but grab his attention. He stood at nearly seven feet tall with a barrel chest and was covered, judging by the smell, in several-sweat matted furs, Charon swallowed. 'I believe I am expected?' He peered up at the shadowed faced.

It snarled at him. 'You are the spy?'

'Spy? Me? No, no, no, no!'

'Then no, you are not. I was told only to allow

entry to the spy.' He smirked.

'Erick, you idiot, stop wasting time. We have to get back.'

'Okay, I take him. Just my little joke.' He laughed and clapped Charon on the shoulder hard enough to make him stumble. Thankfully the other two still had a hold of his arms tightly enough to keep him upright.

'Yeah funny,' one of the guards said. The rolling of his eyes was almost audible. They released Charon's arms and shoved him toward the door guard.

'You. Come!' He let the outer door slam behind them.

As Charon crossed the threshold he felt his limbs grow heavy. It was like a great weariness had settled on him but it was better than his experience at the paint factory. He wondered if these wards were just for him, or if everyone experienced this brand of hospitality? His head spun and he had to put a hand out and lean on a wall for a moment.

Erick stopped. 'Give it a minute. Takes everyone different. Some are sick, others just pass out. You're quite impressive…for a Greek.' Erick grinned and winked. Now they were under the hard UV strip lights Charon could see him properly. He had clearly once been a fearsome warrior. The long white hair and beard were a testament to many years of hard living, and battles fought and survived. His face was a map of lines and ravaged by weather. A long livid scar crossed his forehead and left cheek. His eye, once grey, had turned milky white, but it still shone jovially out at Charon. 'The scar?'

'I didn't like to…I mean…, you're not like me. Were you human once?'

'We all have to die sometime. You of all people should know that.' He shrugged. 'But I can't really answer that. I remember being alive but am told that was not real. I was minding my own business, enjoying Valhalla before we were thrown from our homes. Rejected and forgotten by greedy cowards who wanted more life than was due to them.' He spat on the floor as they walked down a long narrow passage. 'Or did you think it was just your people who suffered from Yahweh's little purge of the immortal realms?' He snorted back a laugh. 'One of the drawbacks of an oral tradition is that our gods and legends did not have the same hold as others.' He paused and raised a scarred eyebrow. 'You look surprised?'

'I just didn't expect...'

'Didn't expect me to be able to string a sentence, let alone understand how this gig works?' Erick grunted, 'Eight centuries of being dead, gives you a great deal of time to catch up on your reading, not to mention one hell of a lot of perspective.' He kicked the door open to a room thick with the smell of sweat, roasting meat, and smoke. The noise was deafening. They had turned the disused space into a longhouse and made it home. Palettes and crates were stacked around a huge makeshift fire pit, over which several spits were being carefully turned. On the other side of what was once the factory floor, a long table had been rigged up from more crates and pallets. On each side scaffolding had been used to make benches which were occupied by men in varying states of consciousness. Charon was guided toward the end of the table nearest the fire. Women bustled past them, stopping only to smile or wink at Erick. When they saw Charon, they turned on their heels and ignored him. His short grey curls and old pale olive skin must have made him stand out a mile. Either that, or they knew what he was.

'Erick! Erick! Get over here!' A voice roared over the din pulling Charon out of his thoughts. 'How long does it take to collect one idiot spy and come back?' He sat on a couple of upturned milk crates covered with a sheepskin and was feeding a pair of ravens chunks of raw meat. 'You think I have all night to wait for you?' The man appeared in his mid to late fifties, but Charon needed no introduction: Odin looked exactly as Hel had described him so many years before. His bearing was unmistakable and Charon had to fight the urge to immediately drop to his knees and declare his undying allegiance. *Get a grip old man, Hades would skin you for less.*

'Go. Get some mead and some supper. You're on guard tonight.' Erick gave a courteous bow and left them in private. Odin indicated him to sit.

'In your presence, sir? I…'

'Sit. Down.' Odin didn't bellow. He didn't need to.

Charon perched on the end of the bench and faced Odin. He tried to speak but the words wouldn't come. He breathed and tried again. 'I apologise for interrupting your dinner, sir...'

Odin stabbed a piece of what Charon assumed to be chicken and leaned back looking him up and down for what seemed an eternity. When he suddenly spoke, it made Charon jump. 'Let's dispose of the social niceties and just get down to the issue at hand, shall we?' He downed the contents of a horn mug by his side and put it in front of Charon, then waved over a serving girl who was holding a large jug. He continued speaking as he ate. 'Let's instead address the fact that you were caught trespassing on my land in the middle of the night.' He stopped speaking as the girl poured Charon a drink. Once she left he resumed 'Let's pretend that you and your companion, what was it?'

'Hermes.'

'Hermes? That's a name?' He shook his head. 'You and your friend were intending to spy on us and disrupted a very important meeting between my representatives and some very powerful beings. Quite a little hobby you are developing there.' He took another bite and spoke with his mouth half full.

'Care to elaborate? In your own time.'

Charon paused for a moment, was there any reason to provoke Odin and tell him that they were planning to film it? He doubted it. His associates, while very dead, were very well armed. No, he would leave that bit out and hope to Hel, that he couldn't read minds. 'Curiosity. Boredom. Take your pick. It's not like I knew the purpose of that meeting the other day. I just run the desk and give people directions.'

'Fair enough, but you were heard discussing it, in public, loudly and have been warned off more than once.'

'By you?'

'Not always. I believe the Fae had a hand in it too.' He took a swig from a bottle of Newcastle Brown Ale and winced as he threw it at a heap of other bottles in the corner. 'Your intentions are, according to them, noble but misguided. For that reason alone, I will not have you or your friend executed for interference. You know the rules. As a leader, I have rights.' Odin gave a half smile. 'Look, don't worry, from the Fae, that's as good a compliment as you can ever hope to expect. They barely tolerate us. To them, the likes of you and I are merely interlopers and intruders, and that makes us a threat no matter how well behaved we are. I wouldn't say we are allies with them, but it's generally safer to be on good terms.'

'It's not like we had a choice... So many of us didn't even survive the crossing, let alone a millennium in the mortal realm.' That bet had come with a high forfeit.

'You don't have to tell me that. I was there. I will answer your questions but you must promise that what you know will go no further than you and your friend. Can you make that promise for him? If you are not certain that you can trust him to keep quiet, you must keep what I tell you to yourself.' Odin's blue-grey eyes met Charon's. His face was an almost unreadable wall, but the jovial smile had gone. He was dead serious and Charon knew only too well what he could do to those who crossed him.

If Charon was being brutally honest he was not at all certain that he could promise on Hermes' behalf. He was known to tell secrets if he saw an advantage to it. 'Very well, but I need you to make me a promise too.' Charon saw no reason that this encounter should be so one-sided. A nod from Odin signalled his agreement. 'I need your assurance on two counts. Firstly, that you will tell me what you know directly. I don't have time for riddles or half-truths. Secondly, I want you to promise that once I have this information, neither you nor your associates will attempt to harm or obstruct us in our actions from now on.'

Odin roared with laughter and clapped Charon on the shoulder. 'You are a very funny man. I will promise you only that I will tell you what I can, but I will be succinct.' This, Charon noted, was not the same as all that he knew. 'I cannot promise that you will not be harmed as I am not the orchestrator of the coming disaster. As noble as your intent may be, if you get too close there will be consequences. Only you can decide if the risks are worth the prize.' He waved the serving girl back, took the jug and sent her on her way. 'Charon, you are not a foolish man - Hel told me as much - but this is not your fight. You are dealing with forces you cannot begin to comprehend.'

'I understand that Ra has decided to flood the planet and re-join Osiris to escape what is coming and because he has decided that he cannot beat it he's going to run away. He didn't say it outright but I remember his promise. It doesn't end well. I can't let him take away the choice to fight or flee from the rest of us. He hasn't even told the other gods the real reasons behind his decision. He lied and told them that he's bored.'

'I see. This might be why I was not invited to attend. You see, I was the one who warned Ra. I wanted to tell all your leaders but I thought it would be unlikely that I would be believed alone and I was assured that he would deal with it. So, the leaders have no idea what is coming?'

'Not a clue.' Charon shook his head. 'Zeus and his brothers haven't even bothered to tell us that Ra is planning to get us all home. Don't take it personally, but they have always put their own interests first. They are not likely to believe me either so there is no point in me warning them, at least not until I know more.' Charon took a sip of his drink and stared at his hands.

'I want you to take this to Zeus, he should know this as it affects us all.' Odin's face was grave and unsmiling. Charon wondered what could possibly make this giant so concerned but it had to be serious. 'You see, the calamity which is set to befall us could well be the deciding war between the gods and the giants. Alone we stand a chance at defeating them again. However, there is a factor which was not in play before.'

'Which is?' *Vikings and their dramatic build ups*, Charon thought impatiently.

'The Titans,' Odin said. 'The Ice Giants[1] have entered into a war pact with the Titans[2].'

---

[1] Big, scary monsters.

[2] Even bigger, scarier monsters. So strong they could only be imprisoned.

A. H. Johnstone

CHAPTER 9

The Message

This information hit Charon like a flying brick and he jumped, falling backwards off the bench. He came to a few minutes later, lying on his back with several people standing around and peering down at him. He felt the back of his head. A lump the size of a golf-ball throbbed furiously. He reached up to take Odin's large, leathery hand and pulled himself to his feet, wobbling a little as Odin guided him back to the bench.

'You took it better than Ra did. Have a drink. You look like you could use one.' A cup of warmed mead was pressed into Charon's hand.

'Angry?'

'Scared. He curled up into a ball, hid under the

table, and started crying. Took us half an hour to get him to come out. I'm not surprised that he has decided he can't win. It probably explains why he hasn't told anyone else, though I am loath to guess as to why he has decided to just wipe everyone out to save his own skin. Cowardly way to do it if you ask me.' Odin shook his head sadly.

'He's even willing to leave his own people to die. The only reason I know this is bigger than him is because I confronted him about his decision to end it all just because he'd had enough.' Charon touched the back of his head again and winced. That was going to hurt in the morning. 'How did the Titans even meet the Ice Giants? As far as I knew the Titans were all still trapped in Tartarus. They weren't happy about it either. They are not to be trusted…'

'And your leaders are? From what I heard, it was the gods who declared war on *them*, not the other way around?' Odin asked, raising an eyebrow. 'You said yourself, none of them has told you about what Ra said. Would you know anything if you had not had the temerity to eavesdrop on their meeting?'

Charon had to take a moment to consider this.

Hades took orders from Zeus, as did Poseidon. Their sisters were pretty much ignored by all three of them. Hera, Demeter and Hestia were gods knew where anyway. Hera had leapt at the chance to divorce Zeus and had levelled every count of adultery and cruelty squarely at Zeus' feet in the process. This had earned her quite a bit of sympathy, and a very healthy alimony award. She would be unlikely to want to talk to them, let alone work with them. Would it be worth tracking them down? None of them was known for sharing information. 'Probably not, but you haven't answered my question.'

'Ha! You tell me. It took Zeus and his brothers to seal them down there so I'd like to know which idiot let them out.'

'Let them out?' Charon was appalled. The very idea that anyone would deliberately release them into the world was terrifying. It meant that whoever did that knew exactly what they were, where they were, and the havoc they could cause.

'Yes. You understand. Good. It took several attempts to explain that to Ra. Look, I am going to be completely straight with you now. Even if I physically could fight them all back, I just don't have the numbers, and the law prevents me from acting alone. I want to get this sorted out before the Council get so much of a sniff of what is going on.'

The laws preventing interference in the ruling of other pantheons were clear and immovable. Odin's desire to alert the other gods was not forbidden, nor was it forbidden to request assistance, but the Council were to have the final say over any plan. They said it was to prevent rash action and exposure of their kind, but Charon suspected it was so they could take credit from the Fae Courts for preventing a disaster. Charon did not envy Odin. He'd had to act but couldn't beat back the Ice Giants with the Titans backing their corner because their very involvement prevented him from acting alone beyond the warning. While ineffectual, he believed he had done his part and tried to warn the Olympians of the coming danger, but from there on his hands were tied. Ra, on the other hand, *had* interfered. His decision to conceal this news to serve his own purpose was espionage and he would have to be dealt with. That would have to wait.

'Did you press the issue of informing the

Olympians?' asked Charon thoughtfully.

'To the point that Ra ceased responding to my calls or messages. He informed me that the matter was now in hand and should be left to him. I had no means to contact your leaders directly or any idea that he had come up with his own 'plan of action.' Odin was clearly unimpressed with this duplicity. 'It explains why I was not invited to that meeting. I would have destroyed his attempt to escape at our expense.'

'You knew about that meeting?'

'Of course. You didn't think the Fae were the only people with spies, did you? Before you ask, no, I won't tell you who they are. They are still useful and telling you would compromise that.'

Charon couldn't argue with that. The rage he felt toward Ra was now reaching frothing point. 'I have no direct access to Zeus or Poseidon,' said Charon. 'I might be able to get a message through to Hades, though I can't see him reacting well.'

'I would be surprised if he did,' Odin said. 'I need you to arrange an introduction. One that won't get back to Ra. If you absolutely need to use Hermes, do, but be careful what you tell him. You might trust him, but I don't. If you have any doubts, don't say anything. Now, it is late and I am tired. You will be escorted back to your friend.'

Charon watched Erick lumber over to them. 'I will need to contact you.'

'Take this,' Odin handed him a cheap throw-away mobile phone. 'There is a contact number already programmed in. Erick, I need you to ensure Charon doesn't get lost on the way out of the building. He has an important job to do for us.' Erick nodded and led the way back to the stairs and out of the hall.

Once they had gone, Odin turned to another figure who had been hiding in the shadows. 'I take it you are satisfied that he was unharmed, Hel.'

'It is cruel to involve him. He does not have the power to survive this.'

'He has more power than you realise, my dear. Power comes in more forms than force or brute strength.'

'Not for this. Odin, he should not be involved. It is not his fight.' She said.

'Do you say that because you care for his wellbeing, and are trying to protect him, or are you hurt that he didn't ask after you, and you want to be rid of him?' Odin looked her in her one good eye.

'That is none of your business!' Hel spat back.

'No matter, but we need to know who or what let our enemies out, how, and why. As it stands, Charon is our only means to that end.'

A. H. Johnstone

CHAPTER 10

The Nurse

The ride back to the old factory was no more comfortable than before. The only difference was the weight of the information Charon carried with him. Someone had released the Titans. As news came, there was little bigger than this. He used the time to think back to before the crossing. An escape from Tartarus was not unprecedented. Long ago, even before the rise of the Olympians, the Cyclopes - the single eyed sons of Uranus, who were locked away because their father was afraid that one of them would usurp his rule - were released by the Titans after they had been falsely imprisoned there by Uranus. This is now known to have been a very bad idea. For all that he had a justified grudge against his deadbeat dad - lived in a cave and slept all day - Cronus turned out not to have fallen far from the tree when it came to crappy parenting. They had managed to rid themselves of a tyrant only to discover that Cronus was as big a despot as his father. *Hands up who didn't see that coming?* thought Charon.

That whole affair led to the emergence of the Erinyes - the judges of the gods, and overseers of divine justice - the Furies; Alecto, Tisiphone and Magaera; the Fates, and the Norns. Basically, they are in charge and woe betide anyone who gets on to their naughty list. It had been they who decreed the law of non-interference after the crossing. Then came Zeus, as spoiled and petulant as any of the Titans who had risked their lives to see him to adulthood, not to mention free his five siblings from the belly of Cronus. Zeus liked to take all the credit for the victory against his forebears but everyone knew the real story. It was just not a good idea to bring it up in his hearing.

As mythical prisons went, Tartarus was not the greatest in terms of high-security. Especially not since Zeus had killed Campe, stole her keys and released the Cyclopes that Cronus had imprisoned after he'd got what he wanted from them. That was when the real trouble started. For a moment, he began to sympathise with Ra's decision to leave the Olympians out of it. *No, this needs to be cleared up once and for all*, he thought. He could think of several suspects who might have had the motive to release them, but would they have had the means?

The van stopped and the doors were opened for him. Thankfully his exit was a great deal more dignified than his initial entrance but it was hardly compensation. 'Where is Hermes?'

'How should we know?' the driver called from the front of the van.

'Shut up, Eadric. Helpful as ever.' He shook his head. 'I'll take you to him. Stay close and only in my footprints or you'll set off the wards again. That won't win you any friends. They take hours to reset.'

Charon did as he was instructed. Luckily the man's boot prints were lit by the flood light above their heads. This time, he could move without being struck down with a mystical heart attack. He still didn't feel right though. What with being thrown around by faeries, setting off magical booby traps and generally ending up on the floor, he'd had enough of being beaten up to last his very long lifetime. Tomorrow, no, today, was a Saturday, so at least he would be able to sleep it off.

It was not long before they reached the old office where Hermes was being held. It looked like it had been ransacked. Had Hermes put up a fight? He sat in an old chair nursing a mug of tea. On either side of him stood a guard dressed like Erick had been, only more heavily armed. They did not look in any mood to joke around. Hermes was being checked over by a matronly woman in a white coat. She was well spoken but had a hint of an Italian accent. He decided not to ask. 'How is he?'

'Stubborn, Mr Charon. Your friend is very stubborn.' She said, tutting and putting her light back in her case. 'I had to call the guards just so I could examine and treat him. That was a nasty cut but there is no major damage and what there is will heal fast. One of the advantages of our kind.'

'Tell me something I don't know. Hang on! Our kind? You're…'

'Like you?' She laughed, 'How would I be here if I were not, Mr Charon?' She patted his arm then looked him up and down. 'It would appear you have your own share of bumps and scrapes. Want me to have a look at that bump?'

'No thanks. It's nothing.'

'Suit yourself. I would recommend that he's not left alone tonight. Keep him at yours tonight and I'll come and check on him later.'

'But you don't know where I live.' This woman was scarily informed.

'Oh, don't I now? Just keep him sat still and give him plenty of fluids.'

'Fluids?'

'*Everyone* should drink plenty of fluids.' The nurse sighed, picked up her bag and left the room. 'Goodnight, Mr Charon. Some of us have beds to get to.'

Charon knelt beside his friend. The blood had been cleaned away and it looked like he had been given stitches. One coat sleeve was rolled away from his wrist and a cannula had been fitted. Probably for painkillers. When it came to treating the gods, it usually took enough anaesthetic to floor an elephant just to take the edge off, and as for the needles... He hoped they had given his friend enough because it looked like that hurt.

'Herm? You awake buddy? It's time to go now.'

'Hmmm, yeah. You okay?' Hermes tried to stand up and swayed. The guards either side caught him and draped an arm each round their shoulders. Charon nodded thanks.

'Never mind that now. Let's get out of here. There is something I *need* to tell you.'

CHAPTER 11

Friends with Forked-Tongues

Hermes choked and sprayed hot coffee over Charon's kitchen table. In fairness, he'd taken the news better than Charon had. He was impressed. The chair had barely rocked at all.

'You okay?' He threw Hermes a cloth and patted him on the back until he stopped coughing.

'A little build up would have been nice.' Hermes croaked, 'Something like 'Good morning, I think you'd better brace yourself, I have some really bad news.'

'I thought I had,' Charon said.

'You didn't even pause!'

'Didn't I?' Charon was sure that he had but didn't

feel it was worth arguing about. 'Sorry. Look, I know you don't think I should get involved...'

'Finally, the penny has dropped!' Hermes snapped as he distractedly mopped up coffee. 'You've only been warned twice. Now you're running errands for a bunch of Vikings? You know they don't trust you right? You're not one of theirs, no matter how cosy you got with Hel.'

'It's not an errand, and it's not like they're pirates... any more. I am one of the only people who knows what's coming. Someone released those creatures and they did it for a reason. What's more, Ra was planning to let us all die just to save his own sorry skin. How do we know it wasn't him who let them out?' He knew this was unlikely. Ra had no access to Tartarus or the realm of the giants. Whoever let them all out had to both have access to Tartarus and be willing to work with a member of another pantheon. Hades had forbidden all but his closest associates from going down there but he'd never posted a guard. *Talk about overconfidence. It could have been anyone.* What Charon couldn't fathom was why anyone would ever let them out. *The Titans hate us. Who would ever trust them?* The noise of a fork handle banging on the table brought his attention back to Hermes.

'Earth to Charon? You still with me? You'd zoned out on me for a moment there. I was asking, why would Ra bother to call that meeting if it was him who released them?' Hermes asked. 'It would be the first thing that would start raising suspicion. You were right the first time. Ra is just looking after himself.' Charon had considered this but added to the fact that Ra did not reveal a larger threat, it had given him pause for thought.

'I don't know. I just don't trust Ra.' Charon could think of a couple of hundred reasons why but he wasn't going to tell Hermes while he was being so obstructive. He couldn't help but notice that Hermes' understanding of the situation was remarkably astute when his sole source of information was Charon, and Charon being a typical member of his Pantheon, had not told him everything. He needed time to think it through by himself. He certainly didn't want to admit that Hermes had raised a valid point about Ra.

'I can help you get a meeting with Zeus. It won't be easy and it could take a couple of weeks to track him down, *but* I will do this on one condition.' His face was a cold mask. When Hermes' face went blank like that, it was a sure sign he knew something important. It meant there was something he was deliberately not saying and it looked like Charon would have to sneak around his friend to get to the truth.

'And that is?' Charon asked.

'Once you have passed the information on, because I agree they need to know, you need to leave this alone. You are kicking a whole hornet's nest of troubles and you are going to get yourself killed. Or worse. Quit prodding, pass on the message, and let the people who have the tools to deal with it do their job.' Hermes sounded serious.

'Worse than dead, huh?' Charon knew he shouldn't joke.

'You know what I mean.'

'Fine.' Could he drop it? Really? Just dropping this would mean ignoring his conscience. It would mean trusting some very unreliable people to put their mistrust and suspicion of outsiders aside for long enough to put these monsters back in their cages.

Making an insincere promise grated on his conscience but until he had told the full story to the people who needed to hear it, and seen their reactions, he could not keep that promise. He couldn't do that until he had the whole story. 'The Nurse who stitched you up is due to check you over later.'

'Don't change the subject, Charon.' Hermes snapped. 'You are meddling with affairs which have nothing to do with you! It's dangerous. How are you going to explain how you know all this? Have you thought about that? You'll have to admit you were listening in.' Hermes was referring to the meeting. The single decision to eavesdrop that started all this nonsense.

Charon sighed, 'I need to take this information to the right people. We're dead if we don't.'

'We? When did this become we?' Hermes had begun to pace. 'I want no part of this.'

'When you refused to let me go up there by myself last night, and you were used to force me to go with those men. I can't sit around and do nothing. Odin can neither act alone nor approach Zeus directly. At least not without going through the Council. He gave me a job to do. I'm not foolish enough not to carry it out. Can you imagine Zeus's reaction if he found out I *didn't* pass on this message?' He paused and added quietly, 'Inaction has cost me too much already.' He leaned back in his chair and picked at his nails.

'Ah. This is about Hel. You're trying to impress...'

'This is not about my ex-wife!' He hadn't meant to snap. Hel was a sore spot and Hermes had just poked it, 'She wasn't even there. For all I know she's already faded.'

'If it doesn't have some benefit to you then why...'

'Hermes, why don't you get it? This is about doing what needs to be done despite the risk. If I don't we're screwed so I might as well try. I'm not looking for accolades or rewards. I just think we should get a say in the way we end. Ra might not be behind the escape but he made a cowardly choice and then withheld the truth so we can't stop him. He also knows that Odin cannot act alone.'

'I get that for some reason, you feel some sense of responsibility toward one set of creatures who don't even think you are real, and another group who know you are but treat you with contempt. And that's only when they bother to acknowledge you at all. I'll get you the meeting, but that's as far as it goes. You drop it and you leave my name out of it. Okay?' Last night Hermes had only reluctantly agreed to help him spy on that meeting. Had the blank stare been fear, as Charon had suspected, or was there something else? Hermes was a known trickster since that whole business of stealing a whole herd of Apollo's cattle, why the sudden caginess? Had 'they' got to him?

'Fine.'

The rest of the morning passed in sullen silence until the Nurse arrived to look Hermes over. If she picked up on the atmosphere she didn't let on. Hermes gave terse one-word answers to her questions about his vision or lingering disorientation, but Charon paid no attention. Having retired to the living room to afford Hermes some privacy he didn't hear anything to prompt his concerns but the speed of his friend's change of heart continued to bother him. He would have to be careful what he said to Hermes in future. He was behaving very evasively and Charon did not want to give anyone reason to change their plans before he could alert the proper authorities.

When the Nurse had finished, Hermes emerged from the kitchen pulling on his jacket. 'I have to go and make those enquiries. This is not something I can do on the phone. Remember your promise, Charon. Once I do this, you pass on your message and leave it alone.'

'I've told you, my friend, I cannot make that promise.'

'I am not saying this as a friend,' Hermes said irritably. 'We've gone way past that. I am giving you an order as a senior deity. Are we clear about that?'

'You can't give me orders…'

'I can. I will do whatever I need to do to keep my friends safe.' On that, Hermes turned and left Charon's house, slamming the door behind him.

CHAPTER 12

The Prophecy

It had been nearly a week since Hermes had left and he had not been in touch with Charon since. On reflection, Charon had decided that pestering Hermes would not help but that did not stop his final words from marching around his head without rest. Hermes had said he would look after his friends. Charon felt he should be taking that at face value, but he couldn't help but sense that he was no longer included in that list of friends. Even so, it was getting urgent. Odin had already chased him about the message twice in the last four days, and asked what was taking him so long. He needed Hermes' help but contacting him didn't seem like such a good idea. The only alternative route to Zeus was The Council.

On his way to work he considered contacting other minor gods. He knew what their reaction would be and they could not be trusted not to try to steal the message and then sell it to Zeus. Many of them still owed him favours. What wouldn't they do to be absolved from those debts? *No*, he thought, *that would be too dangerous and it would risk the information falling into the wrong hands.* Odin didn't know who had released those monsters, and until they did, Charon couldn't be sure who he was dealing with. The wrong word to the wrong person could mean his own eternity in Tartarus. *I promised not to tell anyone but Hermes.* He'd keep that promise, but only because there was little reason to believe that anyone else would react any differently.

His keys jingled as he dragged them from his pocket and opened the door. Hopefully today would go the way of the rest of the week. Aside from being chased by Odin's men, he'd had a wonderfully peaceful week. There had been no more weird texts warning him off, and no visits from irate faeries who didn't know their own strength. However, Charon wasn't happy. It was too quiet, and he couldn't help but suspect that this was the calm before the storm. If this had all been a sick practical joke to teach him to mind his own business, someone upstairs[3] would have found some way to let him know he'd been made to look a fool. Not out of any concern for him, of course. The Olympians still loved to let people know when they'd been tricked for the simple joy of making them feel bad. It was in the same spirit that a mean child pulling wings off a fly laughs when it still tries to take off. *The mortals had had the right idea when they abandoned worshipping us.*

Knowing it wasn't him being made the butt of some bored immortal's joke didn't do anything to help his mood. So far, he'd snapped at the postman, and driven a call centre operative who'd dialled a wrong number to quit on the spot. Like it or not, he would have to call Hermes and sort this mess out once and for all. He decided to use the work line but dialled 141 to hide the number. If whoever had sent him that text message last week had his number, they were probably able to tap his calls, and he didn't want this one to show up on the bill.

It rang several times before someone finally

---

[3] The offices were occupied but he didn't know who/what by. Nor did he want to find out.

picked up.

'IT helpdesk, Cassandra speaking. Who's calling please?'

'Cassandra, it's Charon. Is Hermes there? I need to ask him something.'

'Mr Hermes no longer works here, sir. Can I help you?'

'What! Where's he gone?' This was worrying to say the least. Hermes hadn't mentioned anything about changing his role. As far as he knew, they got placed in a job and were expected to get on with it. Maybe they'd had enough of him killing the equipment. This was too sudden. Someone had got to him.

'How the hell should I know?'

'You're supposed to be…'

'Supposed to be what? All seeing? You know it doesn't work like that and I am sick of people treating me like some sort of walking prediction machine then going off to do the opposite of what I advise. All I know is that he called in Monday. Said he'd had a better offer somewhere else. Can't say that I blame him. Is there anything else because some of us have work to do?'

'No. Thanks. I'll try his mobile.' Charon said weakly. He'd not been prepared for Hermes not being there.

'You do that.' The line died. Cassandra had been prickly since he'd met her but being murdered by your abductor's wife will put a real dent in your armour. She was technically mortal but thanks to her presence in the stories of Troy, and Apollo's sense of humour, she was granted a certain immortality; much to her annoyance - she wasn't a liar. It wasn't her fault nobody listened to her. Well, not completely.

He tried Hermes' mobile several times without success. The final tries told him that calls from his phone had been blocked by that number. Charon put the phone down then sat staring at it for what felt like an hour. It looked like he had no choice. He would have to contact someone else. The trouble was distinguishing between who he could trust and who would be able to offer him any useful help. The entirety of the people on both lists consisted of

Carnus, one of the *very* many sons of Zeus, and a seer.

* * *

It didn't take him long to find Carnus. The seer was not doing well. His thick dark hair was matted and greasy, and greying at the temples, and his clothes were dusty and crumpled. Charon had tracked him down to a park bench in the town centre and found him deeply involved in his philosophical conversation with a pigeon who appeared more interested in a discarded chip than in Carnus. He was a very expressive speaker and as his hands grew more animated Charon could see that his once olive skin was now grey and stretched over his too-thin and cold-blistered fingers. He saw a black bin-liner tucked under his seat and Charon wondered if the man even had any gloves. Winter was no time to be sleeping under the stars. Charon waited for him to finish and the pigeon to depart before he took a seat next to him.

'Ah, Charon. To what do I owe this honour? I was wondering when I would see you. Not dying again am I?' He winked. His eyes were clouded. To the mortal eye, he looked to be in his fourth decade, but Charon knew him to be far older. The last time they had met, Charon had been escorting a very irate seer over the Styx after he had been taken for a spy and murdered by one of the Heraclids. Hippotes had thought that a kill first and ask questions later policy was the best way to greet a stranger approaching their camp. The storm, famine, wrecked fleet, and scattered army, that Carnus had come to warn him about had hopefully taught him the error of his ways. He wore the marks of a troubled life but he had not lost his Greek accent, despite his millennia or more in Britain.

'You know what brings me?' Charon asked. He couldn't have guessed.

'I'm a seer. I know most things, though not enough to keep me out of trouble.'

'I'm looking for some information on how to reach Zeus without…'

'Without going through that gods-awful Council? I know. They've not been much help of late, have they? I'm sorry to disappoint you, but my influence does not stretch beyond pigeons these days.'

'Pigeons?' He felt his voice crack.

'Don't mock. They're smart enough to live off mortals and not have to lift a feather. That last one had just lost his favourite roosting spot and was asking me where the best place to move was.'

'What did you tell him?'

'That home was wherever he decided it was. If one spot was no longer there, he must consider what was most important to him; proximity to food or family. Then he would find a new favourite.'

'And if losing a favourite roost due to the actions of another meant losing all places to roost for all pigeons?'

Carnus laughed. 'The pigeon analogy cannot help you here. Your problem cannot be solved so easily. Pigeons are wise, but short-sighted. They cannot see the bigger picture and their cares are few. You must visit one of the Oracles. They will help... I see you were hoping to avoid them too.'

Charon scowled. He hated that he was so easy to read. Even by a seer. These days his face always betrayed his feelings. The Oracles it was then. Carnus was right; he didn't want to visit them. They gave him the creeps. Those riddles they spoke in gave him a headache and the smoke they insisted on spreading everywhere clung to your clothes for weeks, but even they were less scary than the council. If Carnus couldn't help though, there wasn't anywhere else he could go.

'How do I find them? They don't exactly go out of their way to advertise.'

'Got a pen?'

'I have a phone.'

'Pftt. You disappoint me, Charon. A phone? You've embraced the life of these feckless mortals then? Going out of their way to find new and ingenious forms of idleness…'

'It has a notebook. You really haven't moved on from the luddites at all have you!' Charon had heard the rumours that some of their kind had been involved. For Carnus, the industrial revolution had been the final descent into chaos. He hadn't led the Luddites, but he had sympathised with their cause and had become set in his ways ever since. Charon had not put much stock in those rumours until he'd had to hunt Carnus down for this little chat. One of the conditions of their settlement when they had made passage to the mortal world was that they were 'not to get involved' in human affairs. They were certainly not supposed to draw attention to themselves, so advising and assisting the Luddite rebellion had broken about every rule in the book. If the Council had been able to shove Carnus back in his box they would have done it in a second. As it was, they had to make do with an indefinite suspension. Unfortunately for Carnus, the Council's idea of indefinite lasted an awfully long time.

'I was never one of you. Wasn't really one of them either. Even in my life as a human,' Carnus said. The resentment was plain in both his voice and his face. 'Seers never are. Spend too long with a foot in both worlds and you see how well you fit in.' He turned to meet Charon's eyes. His milky eyes were fixed on Charon, but it felt like they were looking straight through him. 'You think I liked the idea of being dragged back here after being dead for more than a millennium? Ha! First there was that bet, then I let myself be seduced by the promises of that damnable council. Human vanity is what got me into this mess. I figured a healthy dose of rebellion would get me out, but then I've never been so good at predicting my own future.' He patted Charon on the shoulder and continued. 'I bear you no ill will but you'll have to excuse an old man's griping.'

'Some of us aren't ready to go,' Charon said and exhaled slowly. In his rush to heroically stand up to Ra and the others, he'd not considered people like Carnus. Genuinely exhausted, with little to hold them here other than the Council having neglected to release them. Carnus had few stories but they had decided his skills would be useful to them. Then one day they just stopped listening. 'You know where I can find these Oracles?'

'Yes. There's a Psychic Fayre held not far from here on a regular basis. One of the Oracles has managed to wrangle a spot in the cricket club. It's on the London Road. You'll know her when you see her. She's the only one there who doesn't appear pretentious. Nice girl, bit vague. Always has a smile and a cup of tea for old Carnus.' He watched as

Charon tapped the address and the date of the next fayre into his phone. He showed him the screen to check he had them down correctly.

'There's no point showing me that. I can't read it.'

'You've never learned to read?' Charon asked.

'Not in English. Greek served me well enough while I lived. I only learned to speak English so I could understand Chaucer. That was when this language had poetry in its heart. But now?' He huffed. He never completed that sentence as he began to cough violently. Deep, racking coughs that shook not only him but the bench. When the fit subsided, Charon offered him the bottle of water he had in his pocket for which Carnus could only nod his appreciation. When he finally sat up Charon noticed that his lips were tinted with flecks of blood.

'You're ill? We're not supposed to be able to get ill!'

'After the thing with the Luddites, I ended up in one of those cotton mills, and like so many others I ended up with fibres in my lungs. Well, it was that or starve. Unlike them, I can't die from it, what with being dead already.' He proffered the bottle back at Charon who gestured that he should keep it. 'Enough questions now. Let me have my peace.'

Charon decided to grant the man his wish. He stood, walked a few steps but then stopped. 'If you need anything let me know.' There was no answer. He turned to see if Carnus was okay, but the bench was now empty aside for some dead leaves. The seer, and his belongings, had vanished.

* * *

The next fayre was on Saturday. Charon had spent a fractious two days hoping that the Oracle would be able to help. If she was the real thing he knew he would end up having to decipher some painful riddle. He had been waiting by the doors for the fayre to open just so that he could get in and out as fast as possible but the event organisers did not share his sense of urgency. A lengthy queue of mortals had gathered behind him, circling round the car park. Surely, at least one of them would have been expecting his arrival, but the stall holders who recognised him all seemed surprised at his presence. Judging by the scowls and furtive looks some of them were giving him, they were the genuine article. One of them even had the audacity to wave burning sage at him as he passed her stall. Charon understood now why Carnus avoided these places.

Eventually he asked to be directed to the Oracle. An old woman who was slowly shuffling a Tarot deck pointed to the back of the hall but not before dealing him a card without looking up. It was The Tower[v]. He shuddered. It came to something when even a deck of cards was telling him to keep his head down and just accept whatever happened to him. Charon made his way toward the back of the hall. She really was travelling light. There was no table, no flouncy hangings, just a tripod and a small fire bowl which a young woman of approximately nineteen years was struggling to light. She was dressed in a grey tracksuit and pink trainers, her dark hair was scraped into a tight bun on the top of her head, and she was heavily made up. Her eyebrows had been plucked to two pencil line arches giving her a permanent look of amused disdain. Was this her? She had to be an assistant?

'Yeah, what ya gawpin' at? Aint you never seen a tripod before?'

'Sorry, I was looking for the Oracle'

'That's me. What d'ya want?' She snapped pink gum and continued trying to light the fire bowl.

'Can I offer some assistance?' The offer of help seemed to soften her for a moment. As one who was also not accustomed to offers of help, he understood how this might take her by surprise.

'Nah. S'alrigh', bu' cheers for the offer. Greg's out the back movin' the car. Nearly got caught on double yellers and we can't afford another fine. He normally deals with all the mystical shiny stuff to impress the public. I don't see the poin' if I'm bein' honest. I mean, *I* don't need it but punters expect a show. I draw the line at wearin' a dress. Especially one tha' looks like some grandma's net cur'ains.' She'd almost spat the word 'dress'. Charon almost smiled but the girl's persistent dropping of 't's and 'h's made him wince. 'What's so funny?' she snapped.

'Nothing. You're just not quite what I expected. That's all.'

She grinned. 'I never am. Is this gonna take long love, cos I've got payin' customers comin'.'

'Aren't I paying?'

'In a way. I always consult for you lot in exchange for favours. Sometimes a favour is more valuable than money, bu' we all have to ea'. I want two things from you. The first is the truff'.'

'Truff?'

'Yeah. That thing where you don' tell me a load of tall tales about what my info is gonna be used for.'

'Oh, the truth. I'm not sure how much I can say. I'm sworn to secrecy but Carnus said you could help me?'

'With wha'?' She laughed, 'Look, I aint some creepy seer with the whole universe in my head. You actually have to ask me a question, but I can tell when someone is 'aving me on so you might as well tell me straight.'

'Okay.' Charon paused. 'I have to pass on a very important message to someone but the Council can't find out. The problem is I can't find this person without poking around.'

'Naughty, naughty. Keepin' secrets from The Council,' she taunted in mock horror. 'Must be serious if you're on the run from that lot.'

'I'm not 'on the run'. I just don't want to involve them. They are not helpful. Too concerned about risking exposure and breaking the settlement conditions to do what is needed. I can't go into it here. You'd not believe me anyway, but if I can't get this message through, the ire of The Council will be the least of our worries.' He paused and breathed deeply. 'How do I contact Zeus?' He had obviously spoken more loudly than he expected to because he could have heard a pin drop as everyone had stopped talking and were now glaring at the pair of them.

The girl rolled her eyes and spoke loudly to the room, 'Oi! You lo', mind your own bleedin' business will ya, this is a priva' conversation!' The spectators went back to arranging their stalls and talking amongst themselves, but Charon was certain that the topic of their conversation had now suddenly changed to them. She took his arm and led him behind a large display board, 'Are you *mad*? What d'ya wanna get mixed up with that lot for?'

'I have an urgent message. I must pass it on,' Charon hissed back. He was finding his temper fraying. He had been holding on to this message for more than a week and had no idea what was going on other than he was going to be in big trouble if he didn't pass it on soon.

She looked at him through narrowed eyes and pursed her lips. 'Fine. I'm convinced your intentions are honourable. It's none of my business, but from my experience, nothin' good *ever* comes from getting involved in god business. They get you to do them a favour and before you know i' you're being sacrificed on your own altar.'

'Sorry...?'

'Never mind, sore point. And stop saying you're sorry! You're takin' a massive risk for them and I don't think you are gettin' anything in return. Am I right?' Charon nodded. 'You seem like a decent bloke, and I've been around for a damned sight longer than I look like I 'ave, so here's some free advice. This lot in here are mortal which means they are dangerous, at least as far as the Council are concerned. Most of them are total frauds and wouldn't know a psychic vision if it jumped up and bit them on the bum. Others, like Minnie at the Tarot tables, are legit and could do you some proper damage if they decide you are trouble. My point is, you don't know who is listening so keep your bloody voice down! The Council would've skinned me for risking exposure like that.' Charon thought back to the first warning text. He'd already been heard, and warned, by the Fae to watch his step. It was turning out that 'stealthy subterfuge' did not appear in his skillset.

'Can you answer my question in a way that *I* can understand it?'

'Not unless you happen to be versed in Oracular prophecy. 'Ad a crash course at the college have we?' she winked. 'I tell it as it comes to me.'

'Very clever.'

A voice called from the other side of the screen, 'Zoë? Where have you gone this time? You best not be having another crafty fag, woman. You know the nicotine suppresses your visions.'

'That's just Greg. Short for Gregorios.' She rolled her eyes and pulled Charon back round to the other side of the screen to the tripod.

The face of the man who stood waiting would not have been out of place on a vase, but his clothes and hair gave him the appearance of a man who had given up trying to keep up with current fashions in 1953. His straight nose, olive skin, and mess of swept back and oiled curls instantly gave away his Mediterranean roots, but this was coupled with tightly fitted jeans turned up at the ankle with red converse trainers, a plain white shirt which hugged his torso, and the sleeves were rolled to the shoulders showing off his muscular arms. A leather motorcyclist's jacket had been dumped on the chair next to the tripod. It wasn't much but even this view was attracting the attention of many of the ladies in the hall. 'Greg was my priest many moons ago. Now he's my man with a van.' She saw the disapproving look on Greg's face and appeared to only just realise she was still holding Charon's hand. She patted his arm and released him. 'Don't worry, Greg. It's only Charon.' She laughed at his surprised expression. 'Wha'? You didn't think I wouldn't recognise ya, did ya?'

'Yeah. I know who he is. What's he want here?' Greg, still eyeing him suspiciously, held out a hand to Charon who took it cautiously and Charon felt about as welcome as a scorpion in the bathtub. Priest or not he was not to be trifled with, and if the man's handshake was anything to go by, he stayed in shape. The grip was a clear warning to Charon but he was sure the feeling in his fingers would return in time. Charon let his eyes flare and Greg looked away first. His dark curls shook as he turned back to Zoë, 'Lit the bowl yet?' He released Charon's hand and put his own in his pockets.

'Nope. It won't light for me.'

Greg smiled and shook his head, 'Lighter?'

She tossed him the pink disposable she'd been struggling with earlier. 'Be my guest.' She smirked. 'Once that's lit I'll do my thing, but first, I need you to understand that owing me a non-specified favour is no joke. I *will* claim it, and you will be obligated to honour that price. Clear?' Carnus had neglected to offer this little gem of information. *Seers, Soothsayers, Oracles, all the bloody same*, he thought, and he was promising to owe one of the

Sisters - possibly the first - 'a favour' in exchange for a riddle that he would have to go and decipher on his own. He knew he didn't have a choice but that didn't make him feel any happier about it.

'Fire's ready.' Greg said, still eyeing Charon.

'Give me two minutes.' Zoë leaned over the bowl, staring into the flames and breathing deeply.

'Oi! You want me to write this down for you?'

'Yes but no embellishments please. I need it exactly as she says it.'

'Of course.' He looked offended. Greg took a battered reporter's notebook and yellow Bic biro, which had apparently been repaired with several feet of yellowing sellotape, out of a collapsible crate by his feet and perched on the high stool next to the tripod. 'It looks like she's ready to go. Open your ears, ferryman.'

Zoë stepped away from the bowl swaying slightly. Tears streaked her cheeks, and Charon wasn't sure how much was soot and how much was eyeliner. Her blue eyes had darkened almost to black. Suddenly she threw out her arms and her head tilted back until Charon was sure that she would be unable to speak. A hot wind which seemed to have come from nowhere whipped around her, upsetting flyers, and cards were sent flying all around the hall. People ducked for cover as candles were blown out and hangings billowed against their pins. This was obviously not something even the regulars had seen before. Charon backed against the wall and tried to shield his face from the uncomfortably hot wind. Now he understood why she said she didn't need the window dressing.

Finally, she began to speak in a hoarse, rasping whisper.

'Danger bodes where ice meets flame and untrue servants show their colours.

Underneath the canopy of death on the ancient crescent island,

Wise, winged serpents taking their final rest shall provide answers.'

A. H. Johnstone

CHAPTER 13

The Aftermath

What Zoë had seen had shaken her to her core. Once the hot wind and the fire in the tripod had died, she collapsed against Greg who rushed to catch her. Her nose was bleeding. One of the ladies from the rune table barged past Charon with a box of tissues as Greg helped her into the chair, 'Zoe!' he snapped his fingers in front of her face. 'Zo, stay awake love'. Zoë was now sobbing and delirious with grief and fear.

Charon stepped aside to avoid the chaos of fussing mediums, apothecaries, tarot readers and a distraught oracle and realised even his legs were shaking. Was this fright? Shock? After all he had seen in his long years, it took a lot to shock him. He considered quietly disappearing with the prophecy and trying to decode it himself but he couldn't bring himself to abandon her. He felt responsible for her pain and fright. Not that he knew much of this sort of thing. For all he knew, this was the standard reaction to conversing with the gods. It occurred to him then, that he hadn't even asked who she was trying to channel. No. He couldn't just leave.

In a bid to feel useful, and to make up for some of the fright he had caused, he made his way to the small kitchen and helped himself to one of the neatly laid out cups for tea and coffee and a jug of water, much to the consternation of the women running it. He glowered at them and gestured back at the crowd of people now looking after Zoë. It was unlikely that anyone could have missed that little display so a cup out of place was hardly a priority. Another woman came in, nodding her approval when she noted the water and the cup in his hand. She looked him straight in the eye without fear or contempt and beckoned him over to the back door.

'You know who I am, madam?'

'I know. I know what she is too. What I want to know is what you want and why. How much do you understand about what she just said?'

'Not much. I'll have to think about it but I am running out of time.' He looked through the serving hatch at the crowd looking after Zoë. 'Will she be okay?'

'She's in good hands. Leave her to Greg and the others.' She smiled, 'You're not like the others, are you?'

'Madam?'

'Not consumed with rage and jealousy. Not forever trying to get one over on others of your kind. Nothing to prove.'

'I'm not sure I have a kind.' This was true. As there was only ever one of him and he didn't experience any form of infancy, he was almost certain that he had come in kit form. All he remembered of the time before was being a servant. Nobody else seemed to remember him having parents either. Even Cerberus had parents for crying out loud. Not that it mattered now. 'Not to be rude but, do I know you?'

'Unlikely. In my time, I was known as Wadjet[vi]. You and I would have mixed in very different circles. Back to business. Charon, what are you doing here?

Have you any idea how many humans witnessed that? If the Council hear of this...' She tutted and folded her arms.

'Carnus sent me here. I didn't realise it would be so... conspicuous. I have been tasked to pass on a very important message but I cannot find the person I am supposed to pass it on to. I was trying to maintain a level of discretion but now everyone is going to know I'm on some sort of mission. I only came to see if she could tell me where Zeus was hiding these days.'

'I'm sorry I can't help you. I don't think Zoe can tell you either. Carnus is a foolish old man to send you to such a public place. He'll expose us all.' She patted his hand. 'You leave him and this mess to me. There is good reason that the oracles are supervised and this has just about broken every rule going. It'll take me hours to convince this lot they were just seeing things.'

Charon smiled ruefully, 'The Fae have already voiced their displeasure over my carelessness.'

'I heard. Which is why I will deal with this. The Fae might be full of hot air but they will not tolerate more mistakes, and they can cause very real harm. You need to get that prophecy from Greg and then make yourself scarce.'

* * *

Charon stared at the crumpled piece of paper with the scrawled prophecy on it and nursed his third pint. After several hours of trying to decipher the note and failing to make any sense out of it he had given up and sent a message to Hermes. 'Danger bodes where ice meets flame,' was clearly referring to the Ice Giants working in cahoots with the Titans, but he knew that already. He wasn't sure if the reference to servants was plural for a reason but it was certainly logical to assume that more than one person had released the Giants and Titans, as none but an Olympian would have had access. The Ice Giants, too, had been off limits to any but the Norse. Even Yahweh had not been foolish enough to release the prisoners of the Gods.

The pub door opened. Hermes sauntered in like

he owned the place and joined Charon at the table. Charon took Hermes' opting out of buying a drink as a clear signal that he had no intention of staying or drinking with him. Again, his face was an impassive mask. *No,* thought Charon, *not blank this time. He's angry.*

'What do you want?'

'Good to see you too. When I couldn't get hold of you about meeting Zeus I went to see an Oracle....'

'You what!' Hermes visibly tensed. 'Are you trying to get yourself in trouble?'

'Calm down and lower your voice. I was running out of time, you were nowhere to be found and Odin has been on my case.' He passed Hermes the note. 'I can't work out more than the first part. I was hoping that you would understand it. Do you want a beer?' He decided not to ask him why he had left his position.

'No. I don't have time,' Hermes murmured as he read it through. 'Which oracle gave you this?' he asked, looking at the note as if it was about to bite him.

'Her name is Zoë. Carnus knows her so I assume she's an Oracle to Zeus.'

'And she couldn't just tell you?'

'Wouldn't. Apparently, it doesn't work like that. Whatever she saw, she took a serious turn for the worse. I couldn't get near her or her priest for clarification. It was all very… public.'

'You'd better hope the Fae courts…'

'Apparently, it's being dealt with.'

'Who by?'

'Someone in charge of the oracles.' It occurred to Charon that Hermes was more interested in who had heard the prophecy than the prophecy itself. Was Hermes avoiding the question? It wasn't the first time he'd been cagey over this. How far would he go to keep 'his friends' safe?

'Suit yourself. It's probably not important anyway.' Hermes yawned hugely. 'The ancient serpent could be referring to the dragons and the only crescent shaped island I can think of off the top of my head is Japan. I think it's a waste of time. As far as I'm concerned, they are already extinct.'

'It won't be easy to find them then.'

'You could try the forest at the foot of Mount Fuji. I've heard whispers about those woods. If you go, as you appear determined to keep digging, do not go without an offering. It must be something personal to you. Is there anything else?'

'I need to pass on this message. Have you been able to get hold of Zeus?'

'Yes. He wants a word with you too. You must present yourself at five o'clock on Tuesday. The conference room at Windsor Court at the Kingsmead Business Park. Zeus doesn't want you reporting the location of his actual place of work back to potential enemies. Word to the wise, he is not happy that you have demanded his attention like this.'

'I demanded nothing. I sought a moment of his time to pass on a message. What the hell have you told him?'

CHAPTER 14

The Green Haired Barman Isn't So Green

'Nothing to worry about.' Hermes looked up from the note. His voice was level but his face was blank again. Charon felt his heart racing but deliberately decided to still his breathing. Courting trouble at this point would be a distraction and lose him an ally, assuming he hadn't already lost him. He realised then that Hermes was not looking at him but over his shoulder at the barman. It was the same one that had been behind the bar when he and Hermes had had their initial catch-up. The night when Charon's boredom had ended. How he now longed for a return to those uninteresting times.

Without a word, Hermes stood and approached the bar. Charon assumed at first that he had changed his mind and gone to get a drink. That was until Hermes reached over the bar, grabbed the boy by his shirt front and dragged him over the bar scattering glasses in the process. Several continued to roll and smashed on the floor and into the sink behind the bar. Charon leapt out of his chair and moved to separate the pair. Hermes had punched the boy so hard he had crumpled to the floor and was in the process of dragging him back to his feet. By the time Charon had got there to separate them, Hermes had him bent backwards over the bar.

'Hermes! Stop!' Charon shouted. 'What the hell are you doing!?' He planted a hand squarely on the barman's chest holding him firmly in place and the other was held out, warning Hermes to keep his distance. Charon didn't want him wandering off without finding out what had happened between the boy and Hermes to inspire such an extreme reaction. What he had not expected was the boy's laughter. Hermes moved to take another swing at him but Charon blocked the punch. 'That's enough!'

'He's a stinking spy, Charon!' Hermes shouted, pacing and running his fingers back through his hair.

Charon rounded on the boy. 'Is this true?'

'What if it is?' The boy laughed again as he wiped green blood from his nose with the back of his hand. It left a smear across his cheek.

'Well,' Charon's mouth tightened, 'The way I see it I have a choice, and in that so do you.' His grip on the boy tightened against his struggling. 'You can either tell us who you are and who you work for and, if I like the answer, I will continue to prevent Hermes from doing you any more damage. If I do not like the answer…'

The boy ceased laughing but his face was still manic. He had clearly not counted on this. Being caught had probably not figured highly on his possibility list either. Overconfidence is a common ailment. Particularly susceptible are investment bankers, local radio DJs and people who buy lottery tickets on a regular basis. Eyes wide open, he sputtered an answer. 'I'm Robin.'

'Just Robin?' Charon asked.

'He's Robin Goodfellow. He's a puck. Mischief maker and all-round good for nothing, former dog's-body for the Fae. They threw him out but he's trying to worm his way back into their good-books.' Hermes interrupted and tried to move in for another swing.

'Hermes, be quiet. I want to hear it from *him*.' Charon said quietly.

'You trust him, but you're questioning *me*?' The boy asked, as he jerked his head in Hermes direction. Charon did not answer. 'You're wasting your time, you know. There is nothing you can do to stop what's coming.'

'What do you know about what is coming?' This piqued Charon's interest again. Hermes wasn't just angry with the boy. He wanted to shut him up. Why else would he be so angry to see him? What was an exiled minor-member of the Fae to Hermes unless he knew something Hermes didn't want him to share?

'I know who released those monsters, and I know you're looking in the wrong place.' He laughed again. 'I also know that the Titans are just a means to an end.'

'And that end is?' Charon caught a glimpse of himself in the mirror above the bar. His eyes were glowing again and it took all the self-control he had to shove the ball of burning rage rising inside him back down. Anger wouldn't help him. Not here. The boy had also seen his face and nodded frantically. Charon released him. It was more out of disgust at his cynical selfishness than sympathy for the boy. This information would be useful evidence to take to Zeus on Tuesday. He only hoped that Zeus would let him get a word in edgeways.

'The Giants want the Earth for themselves. They have no intention of sharing. Not with you, or the Titans, or anyone else.'

Odd thing to say, thought Charon, he must think we have something to do with it.

'I think whoever released them has already done that.' Hermes interrupted again. This time his voice was shaking. 'Ask him what he's been up to.'

'Shut-up, Hermes! I'm dealing with it.' Charon's attention returned to Robin. 'What about the humans? This is their home. Are you working for the Fae?'

'Collateral damage. The humans don't care, do

they? Just look at what they do to the place. I just go where the money is. Have to eat, don't I?'

'Fine.' said Charon, 'You just tell whoever you work for that we know who you are and that you have been compromised. It is not in my power to kill you myself, faery, but if I catch you spying on me or anyone else again, I won't stop them from taking you down. Clear?'

CHAPTER 15

The Boss Is Not Happy

Tuesday came. Charon had been waiting for almost forty minutes. He knew what this was. Zeus was doing his best to show Charon that he was in charge by keeping him waiting. He was in there, Charon could see him, and Zeus knew he was waiting because it was Zeus who had told him to wait outside until called. It felt like an age had passed already, but at least Zeus hadn't been playing with time the way Ra had. Did Zeus know about that trick? A moment later, a young woman in a navy skirt suit and ridiculously high heels opened the door.

'Zeus will see you now.' She said as she held the door for him and then left the room.

'Thank you.' He didn't recognise her but he sensed that she wasn't mortal. Zeus would sleep with any woman who would let him near her but would never have allowed a mortal to work for him directly. Charon approached the desk cautiously as Zeus sat typing furiously, stopping only to gesture to a straight-backed office chair which he took gratefully and waited for his legs to stop trembling. The desk was empty aside from a mobile phone and a laptop.

Once he was seated, Zeus spoke to him. 'Mr Charon, my word, we *have* been busy.'

'Sir?' Charon tried to swallow but his mouth was too dry.

'Eavesdropping? Unauthorised meetings? Defying direct orders from superiors *and* the Fae courts, and a very public visit to my Oracle.' Zeus leaned back in the high-backed chair and fiddled with the arm. 'Care to explain yourself?'

'I came to deliver a message…'

'Indeed. You are aware that you have broken several Rules of the Council and the Conditions of Settlement, not to mention committing several acts of direct insubordination.' Charon knew that this last one was untrue and so did Zeus. Neither code prevented gods major or minor from interacting. They were written with a view to keep the peace and put an end to the bitter feuding that had contributed to their loss of power and the ability of one god to usurp them all.

'Insubordination sir?'

'Hermes told you several times to stay out of it, did he not?' Charon seethed. Charon realised at that moment that Hermes had told Zeus just enough to curry favour with his father, get himself out of trouble and get Charon into a great deal of it.

'Yes, but…'

'But nothing! We may be stuck here for the foreseeable future but we still have rules, observance of which our existence depends upon. If a superior tells you to do something, you do it.' He leaned forwards, 'Hermes has been instructed to stay away from you. I have also spoken to Ra and apologised for your intrusion the other day. From now on, you go nowhere without my express permission.' It was true that Zeus was obligated under the Conditions of settlement to deal with discipline within his ranks and keep on non-aggressive terms with the other gods. It was not true that they were forbidden from interacting on a non-official basis. It could be said that his involvement was official but then he remembered something about the original meeting. He didn't like having to do what he was about to do. Blackmail was such an unsavoury practice but desperate times called for underhand measures.

'Did you inform the Council? About Ra's meeting and intentions, I mean, not my own actions.'

'That is irrelevant, and don't interrupt.' Zeus' face might have remained stern and foreboding but the quaver in his voice revealed that he knew more than he was saying. Zeus knew he was lying. He knew Charon knew he was lying. *It's easy to spot a liar*, thought Charon. *Most liars make more effort to deflect attention from themselves, or convince you of their honesty, than to prove what they say. They do all they can to discredit those who contradict them. Only real 'professionals' can lie instinctively, and for that to work they must enter a state of semi-insanity and truly believe their own lies*, thought Charon. Central London estate agents, no-win-no-fee solicitors, and many politicians have made good money from this form of lunacy. Charon had seen all of them and most of them had called themselves a 'hero' at some point in their lives.

'Is it?' Charon stood and leaned across the desk as he had in Ra's office. *Time for more parlour tricks* he thought. Charon made the room darken and let his eyes flare in the low light. He no longer had the strength to cast an illusion to make the room appear as the banks of the Styx, but he could still make Zeus feel like they were back down there. It was well known that Zeus hated dark enclosed places, he needed to be able to see the sky. 'I know the Conditions of Settlement as well as you do. I also know the rules of the Council. I *also* know that there were no representatives of the Council in that first meeting. Nor have they been present in any of yours, or Hades' official meetings, for some years. If the council should discover this discrepancy, what would you say would happen? It would be a shame if someone let that slip to the wrong person.'

Zeus went pale. 'I would be relieved of my command. So would Hades.'

'Correct. Would my suspicions be correct, if I were to suggest that the reason you have done nothing to stop Ra, or even warn the Council, is because you would rather hang on to your power for a few more months, than sound the alarm and risk your position by bringing your own misconduct to their attention?'

Zeus gave a half smile 'It's so easy for you to criticise. You've never been more than a gatekeeper.'

'I *am* a gatekeeper. One who knows the comings and goings of everyone who uses that building. I admit I eavesdropped on the meeting and it was probably reckless, but I would not have found out what I am about to tell you had I not remained involved. You, on the other hand, hid in your office and pretended nothing was happening. I still came here to deliver a very important message knowing what it could cost me. You have just tried to punish me for doing what you should have done so that you can keep your own nose clean with the Council. You're no better than Ra.'

'So, you do have a spine after all. What are you planning, Ferryman?' He gave a half smile. If Charon didn't know better, he might think Zeus was impressed.

Charon considered this for a moment, 'If you do

not shut up and let me give you this message I shall pass on everything I know to the Council and the Fae courts. You'll leave me with no choice.'

Zeus raised a perfectly shaped eyebrow. 'Message? What message? What are you talking about?' Zeus seemed genuinely surprised. He looked like he was going to be sick. Charon had expected an outburst of rage so the lack of expected reaction put him off but only for a moment.

'The message I requested this meeting to talk about. I don't know how much Hermes has told you,' Charon said calmly. 'It's likely not to be the whole story, and frankly I don't care anymore, but am happy to explain it myself if you are prepared to listen. Unlike some of us, I honour my promises.' He returned to his seat. Charon considered that he'd either just made the bravest move or stupidest mistake in his long, long life. They sat opposite each other, weighing each other up in silence for several seconds.

Zeus breathed out deeply and pressed the intercom. 'Hestia, please bring us two large cups of coffee. Make it the strong stuff, I think I'm going to need it.' He released the button. 'Okay, Charon. You have my attention. So, if you would kindly get out of my head, we can begin.'

CHAPTER 16

The Errand

Charon decided to begin with the message from Odin. As expected, the news that the Titans had not only been released but were working with the Ice Giants was not welcome and several phone calls later, Charon was surrounded by all six of the head Olympians who listened intently as Charon recounted the details of everything that had happened since the meeting. About Ra hiding away and working to save his own skin without giving anyone a chance to fight back, the strange warnings, the fact that the Fae courts were livid but refusing to do anything in case they exposed their existence. He described his encounter with Odin and being directed to Zoë by Carnus. He patiently answered their questions, knowing they were testing him, but all the while feeling more and more relieved that this information was in the hands of those who could do something with it. Or so he thought.

After much whispering and muttering, none of which Charon's mortal hearing could clearly pick up, Hera rose from her seat and came to stand in front of him holding out a perfectly manicured hand. She was smiling but she still terrified him. He rose and shook it as invited. It would have been rude not to. 'First, I want to congratulate you. Charon, you have been so very brave but I don't quite know how to break this to you.'

'Break what to me?' Charon's heart raced. It was true that since she had divorced her unfaithful husband and gone on to live her own life, her temper was much improved, but this did not mean that she was in any way 'nice'. The gods still granted favours among their own kind and rewarded loyalty but none of them were 'nice'. They didn't *do* 'nice'. Charon had learned from the experience of others that if they at any point appeared to be 'nice', it was time to run very fast in the other direction and not look back. He swallowed.

She took his arm and guided him to the window so they could speak privately. 'Do not worry. You are not in trouble. What you have told us is upsetting but you did what was right. We need you to continue in this ambassadorial role you appear to have carved out for yourself. It would appear you have hidden talents.'

'Not that I am not relieved, but can I ask why? I had expected to be flayed or chained to a rock for interfering.'

Hera laughed and squeezed his arm with her free hand, 'Yes, well these are different times. Your question is pertinent. The reason we need you to do this is what brought you here in the first place.' Charon stared blankly at her. 'Your honesty and compassion for others who as you say have been denied an opportunity to fight back. You have not asked or even suggested that you might be rewarded. You, Charon, and only you, are worthy to be entrusted with this role. My brothers wanted Hermes to do it, despite his conduct, but it is clear he only tells us what he feels will best serve himself.'

'And the prophecy?'

'The one from Zoë? Yes, that helped to corroborate your story.' Hera frowned. 'She might be common and crude, but the girl *is* truthful and *highly* skilled at her job. That's the other reason we need you. The prophecy was given to you so only you can find out what it means. Mind you, Hermes' guesses were more astute than I think even he realises. There is a dragon living in that forest. She is very old and it has been centuries since anyone has seen her. Many believe she is already dead. If she knows anything we must find out what it is. If that prophecy is anything to go by, she is still there and waiting for you. Now, we must hurry. Travel is being arranged as we speak. Too much time has been wasted already. Go straight there and come straight back. I warn you, Charon, this is too important to put in any electronic communication, especially as you seem to have been hacked.'

'Those warnings to stay away weren't sent by any of you?'

'No. Until today I knew nothing. Even of the first meeting but my sisters and I will deal with our brothers.' In that moment, Hestia arrived at Hera's side and cleared her throat.

'Excuse me, Hera? Charon's travel papers have been arranged.' She handed Hera a folder of paperwork and looked on as she flicked through it. 'I had to organise a temporary passport as it appears he has never owned one. A car is on its way to take him directly to the airport. There was not time for us to send anyone to your home for fresh clothing so a case will be waiting for you on the plane.'

'Thank you, Hestia. You are a marvel.' Hera turned back to Charon, 'Remember, Charon. You must come directly back to us with whatever you find out.' Hera passed him the file, escorted him through the door and closed it firmly behind him.

Well, thought Charon, looks like I am going to Japan.

A. H. Johnstone

CHAPTER 17

The Dragon

Charon stepped off the small private jet and was met by a young woman in a smart black skirt suit. He bowed at the waist in greeting which was returned. Her face, half covered by dark glasses, barely moved. Was she like him? As he followed her off the tarmac to a small arrivals lounge, Charon considered what had brought him here. Had it really been two weeks since he'd eavesdropped on that meeting? It must have been.

'Your car is waiting, Charon san.' The young woman who had taken his documents and led him through the immigration process returned and handed them back to him. 'If you would follow me, please.'

He extended the handle of the small cabin

suitcase the other gods had provided him with and did as he was asked. Following her through the crowds in the baggage collection, and out to the front of the airport, where a long black limousine was waiting for him, he wondered if any of these people had the first idea of what was really in those woods. The paint had been polished to a high shine and it gleamed in the winter sunshine. The driver stepped out and opened the door for him. Charon placed his carry-on into the back before turning to the young woman. She was familiar but he couldn't think why.

'Excuse me, Miss, but do I know you?'

'I do not think so. I have not yet passed through your realm.'

'You're alive?'

'I did not say that. Who I am is not important.'

'Will you be coming with me?'

'I cannot. I have not been invited to visit the Lady. Now, you must listen to me. When you get to the forest at Aokigahara, follow the gold thread. That will take you to her. It is very important that you do not stray from that path. There is more than one way to get lost in that forest. Do you understand?'

'Loud and clear.' Charon answered.

'Your driver has been instructed to wait for three hours. If you have not returned by nightfall…' She paused, 'How much do you know of the forest, Charon san?'

'Not much. Why?'

'At this point, it is probably best that it stays that way. I would not like to be the cause of your dishonour. It will take just under two hours to get there. I advise you to rest. Good day.' She gave another small bow before returning to the airport and vanished into the crowd.

Charon shut the door and the car pulled away.

* * *

Two hours later, Charon was woken by a tap on

the window. The car had pulled to the side of the road and the driver was stood by the car waiting. Charon tried the door but it wouldn't open from the inside. The driver let him out. He did not seem at all happy to be parked where he was. Charon wondered what could possibly have made him so uneasy. He reached in for his pack but the jittery driver shook his head and pointed to the uneven forest floor.

It was a mass of roots and moss, and rocks. He was right. Where had he been sent? Charon had never seen anything like it. Or for that matter heard anything like it. Even the Underworld hadn't been this quiet. The trees seemed to absorb sound. There was nothing. No birdsong. No cute scurrying woodland creatures. Even the breeze couldn't get through to rustle the leaves. It took a lot to make Charon feel uneasy, but this place? This place hit all the wrong buttons.

He peered around the tree branches looking for the gold thread. It took some time even with the driver's help, but eventually he found a tuft of gold thread tangled with a handful of others. Charon wasn't surprised. He wouldn't want to go in there without first making damned sure he could get back out again. He checked his watch. It was midday. He had three hours to get in, ask his questions and get back. Peering in, he now understood why he would need that time, and he did not want to know what would happen should he fail to return on time.

'Best get going then.' He said to the driver, who did not look any happier after finding the thread than he had before and started walking.

* * *

Charon was relieved to be doing this in the day time. Even in the light of day the weight of the place closed in around him. He gathered himself and kept walking, holding tightly to the gold thread, it chafed against his sweat covered palm. It had already taken him forty-minutes to reach this point and the end of the path was nowhere in sight. Every step brought him more uneasiness but he couldn't turn back now. How would he explain it to Zeus? *'Yeah, you know that job you sent me on? Well, I chickened out of the walk through the woods and came running home.'* He could see how well that would go down. He was the ancient ferryman of the Styx and here he was trembling. What could happen? Well, he could let go of the thread and never see home again. Charon tried not to think about it.

He walked until he found himself in a clearing. The other end of the thread had been tied to the sign at the base of a huge tree. *'Now what?'* he thought. The only place he was prepared to go was back along the way he came. He couldn't read the sign but there was a telephone number at the bottom. The silence had become oppressive. Checking his watch, he found he had been walking for more than an hour. It didn't leave him much time to find out what he needed and get back out. Getting back out couldn't happen quickly enough.

'I haven't got all day, ferryman.'

Charon jumped and cried out. The voice came out of nowhere and he couldn't tell which direction it had come from. Charon clasped his chest and caught his breath as he turned around in circles trying to find the origin of the voice. There was no sign of anyone. More to the point, how did they know who he was?

'Who said that? Where are you?'

'Here.' A voice boomed from right behind him.

Charon spun round to find himself face to face with a dragon. He jumped back and tripped on a tree root. As he sprawled on the ground and waited for it to cease laughing, he took in the sheer size of the beast. Her head alone was the same height as Charon and covered in pearlescent white scales and trailing blue whiskers. How long she was, Charon had no way of telling. Her white-scaled body was serpentine and wingless, and striated with blue-grey bands. Her head and 'shoulders' were supported on muscular legs which seemed short in relation to the bulk of the rest of her body. Her feet had gleaming black claws on each of the three massive toes. He could only see one pair. She could have had more but he could only see the first fifty meters or so. The rest of her long, slender body disappeared down a nearby chasm. Charon couldn't remember seeing anything so beautiful.

As she lifted her foot and picked her teeth, her head turned and he caught a glimpse of one of her eyes. At some point in her past she had been horribly injured. The left side of her face bore a scar which ran from the top of her head, over the eye and down to her upper lip. The eye was a milky blue pearlescent orb which neither moved nor blinked. The other was blue with an elliptical pupil. She fixed him with her good eye.

'Finished staring?'

'What? Oh, sorry.' Charon climbed to his feet. 'You startled me.'

'I know,' she said. 'That was the idea. You must allow an old dragon her amusements.' She laughed again, but this time it sounded more like racking coughs than laughter. On closer inspection, her scales were in a terrible state. Many were missing and there were patches that looked like an infection had set in underneath. Charon's heart sank. This creature, once magnificent and terrible, was now dying, and was using the last of her time to help them.

'I... I was told you had some information.'

'I have lots of information. What I do not have is time. Be succinct!' she ordered. Her voice seemed to emanate from inside his head. It certainly had not come from her mouth.

'Yes. Pardon me, Lady.'

'Lady? I am a dragon! You think I care for your human airs and graces? Pfft.' She limped around. Corralling him, so that the only way back to the path was either to climb over her or wait until she allowed him to leave. Charon was not prepared to make a bet on her reflexes.

'Sorry—'

'Stop apologising! You are here for a reason? Fulfil your purpose.' She half slithered – half limped - around the other way, 'and stand up straight! Your posture is terrible!'

'The Titans have been released.' He didn't know how else to put it. How would you put that gently?

'And?' She sounded bored and irritable.

'And? They are working with the Ice Giants!'

'Humph. Too bad for you.' She licked at a sore patch which shed more scales, 'I warned you all centuries ago that this would happen. I told Zeus myself that locking away an enemy he could not defeat through wit or valour had no honour. So, what does he do? He sends a servant along to pick my brains when it all blows up in his face.'

'I... I...'

'I... I... I...' the dragon mocked 'Of course you didn't know. Why would you know? You think everything that went on was recorded by your precious poets? Pah! You don't have the first idea.'

'Please. If there is anything you can tell us it would be appreciated.'

'That'd be a first!' she grumbled. She fixed him with her good eye again. 'Sit down, young man and open your ears. I will not be stopping for questions!'

* * *

The dragon's words were harrowing to say the least. She could not give names as her foresight did not work that way. What she could tell him were flashes of feeling and interpretations of blurred visions. She told him of a great battle to come, of the forces that had been released which could either destroy them all or restore them to glory. She told him of enemies who hid in the shadows of allies, and allies found in unlikely places. Most importantly, she warned him that Zeus's time would come to a permanent end if her word was not heeded.

Charon looked at his watch. He now had less than an hour to return to the car. The dragon was lying exhausted in front of him. Her voice had barely been a whisper by the time she had finished telling Charon what she knew about Ra, and giants, and Titans. As she spoke and coughed he attempted to comfort her, stroking her battered scales and offering water from his bottle. There was only one thing more he could do for her. The mortal realm could no longer sustain her --- there was not enough belief left -- but he did not see why she must endure this agony.

'Thank you. Your message will be carried. Is there anything more I can help you with?' He stroked the now wilting whiskers as he spoke to her and imagined how impressive she must have once been.

'Hmm?' she said, sleepily and coughed again. What Charon assumed was blood dribbled from the corner of her mouth. It was thick and black. He wiped it away with his handkerchief.

'Charon...?'

'I'm here.'

'I have one last thing to say.'

'Save your strength.'

'Save it for what, man? I'm dying. I knew that before you and your kind passed to the mortal realm that my time would come. There was not enough belief for all of us. You know better than anyone that death spares nobody.'

'I've met her. You'd have liked her.' He continued to stroke her whiskers.

'I'm sure I would, ferryman.' She coughed again. 'Be careful in whom you place your trust, many a seasoned soldier has been fooled by silken words spoken with a forked tongue.' With that, she closed her eyes and didn't move again. Charon had considered using his power to ease her way, but she had not asked him to. What right did he have to decide for her? If she had asked him to help he would have done so in a heartbeat but now it was too late to give her something in return. He closed the dragon's one good eye and gently kissed the bridge of her nose.

As Charon walked away from the dead dragon, tears slid down his face for the first time in living memory.

A. H. Johnstone

CHAPTER 18

After the Dragon

Charon sat outside Zeus' office waiting to be shown in. He'd have thought that with all the urgency that he'd been sent to Japan, they might have been more prompt about letting him speak his piece. More power games? Did he care? At this point, the answer to the latter was 'not really'. With any luck Zeus would see him, and deal with this mess so that he could go home and his life could go back to normal. *Could it? Surely, there would be consequences?*

The door opened and Hera stepped out. 'Charon. Thank you for coming.' She said as if it had been a choice. He had been ordered to come straight back. For the last seventy-two hours, he had had a maximum of four hours of sleep, learning the hard way that he could not, no matter how exhausted, sleep on aeroplanes. It had not put him in a good mood. 'Please, come in.'

Charon rose and followed her through. The Olympians were all there, sat along one side of the long conference table like a panel of judges. Hera led him to the chair in the middle of the other side of the table. A large jug of cold water had been laid for him and dressed with ice, lemon and mint. As if that would be enough to tempt him. He was not prepared to eat or drink anything given to him by these people. Who knew what the lemon and mint were covering up? He took his seat and waited for Hera to hand out clipboards before returning to her own. It had been very deliberately put on the right of Zeus.

Charon wasn't fooled. There was no way Zeus could know what he had been told in that forest. He hadn't told another living soul. Zeus was still trying to give the impression that he knew what he was doing. Like he could use words rather than hurl lightning around. This was straight out of Ra's book of '*How to look important and impressive in the mortal world without actually doing anything.*' It was window dressing. Even now, Zeus had to make the point to everyone that he was in charge. From the expressions ranging from boredom to outright contempt on the faces on the other side of the table, they were no more impressed than he was. *Here goes nothing,* thought Charon.

'Ladies and gentlemen, I bring you some disturbing news, but first it brings me no joy to tell you that the dragon of the Aokigahara forest died imparting what I am bound to tell you.' There were gasps around the table. 'We owe it to her memory to use this information wisely.' He paused to allow the whispering to stop. 'I come here only to impart this information. Then I shall take my leave.'

'You'll do as you're told!' Hades snapped, 'If you'd just done your job—'

'If I had 'just done my job' you would know nothing of this. You would have no idea what was coming and no idea how to stop it!' Charon surprised himself. He'd always been slightly terrified of Hades. The last two weeks had shown him that the people who claimed to be his betters were nothing to be afraid of. Even after their expulsion from the mortal realm, they cared more about appearances and defending their own reputations than doing anything to earn them.

'I have complied with your instructions – yours and Odin's - and not gone to the Council but it occurs to me now why it is that you want to keep it from them. They have the power to strip you of your own power and influence, and you fear that over anything else.' They sat in shocked silence. This was probably the first time that they had been faced off by a servant. 'The titans got out on your watch. Not only did they get out on your watch, but you didn't even know they were gone until I told you!' his voice was rising now.

'How dare you—' Hades chimed in again.

'I dare because I have nothing to lose and everything to gain, sir! Whose realm were they in when they escaped?'

'Mine.'

'And who was guarding them?'

'The seals on Tartarus are—'

'Impenetrable? Given the fact that they have escaped before, surely you know better than this?'

'Yes but—'

'But nothing!' Charon bellowed in a voice so deep and hollow it had serifs. His eyes flashed blue and the panel of gods saw a glimpse of what lay under the human form he had been given. 'They were left without guards in a realm they had already escaped from before. The only thing which amazes me more than the stupidity of that scenario, is your pig-headed refusal to accept any responsibility. Anyone could have let them out!'

'Take your seat, ferryman,' Zeus warned.

Charon's rage was so great that he hadn't realised he was standing and the chair was now lying on the floor behind him, but he decided to use the moment. His head snapped around to Zeus and felt his own dormant power crackle under his skin. His eyes flared with electric blue light. 'You dare try to silence me? The dragon warned Zeus. Did he tell any of you that? Long ago. She warned him of the risks of imprisoning those he feared. They had committed no crime other than being stronger than he could ever hope to be so he felt threatened. He could not defeat them, not even with all your help, so he locked them way in the darkest parts of the world so they could not threaten him anymore. It wasn't to protect you all from your father, it was to hide from his hypocrisy. The dragon warned him that imprisoning perceived enemies will only create real ones. That it was only a matter of time before they would break out and destroy us all. Now they have allies. What have you to say, 'Titan slayer'?' He spat the words 'Titan slayer'.

Muttering erupted down the line as Hades and Zeus simply stared at him. Their eyes were black with rage but they could do nothing to him. The other gods wanted to contact the Council but Hera cleared her throat.

'Thank you, Mr Charon, your speech has been quite illuminating.' Her eyes sparkled, but he doubted this was from grief or shock. Her own ambition was notorious and she clearly saw an opportunity to take her family in hand. Would she use it to settle old scores? She was unlikely to take it out on him. Charon had just handed her what she wanted; two of her brothers had proven themselves inadequate to the task of keeping their people in line. That only left Poseidon to stand against her, and Charon did not want to be around for *that* power struggle. However, if the Council found out about any of this, Hera and

Poseidon's power grab would come to nothing. Charon shook his head. Even with the apocalypse looming, they still only cared about their own power.

'Have you not heard a word I have said?' Charon asked quietly. 'You think the Titans care about your petty bickering? You think they are going to wait until this is all sorted out? You are going to have to swallow your pride and accept the help of Odin and his people, or we are all done for.' There were more whispers and shocked gasping at the very idea of cooperation. He wasn't getting through. What would it take?

Charon was no longer the focus of the room. Most of the others were locked in bitter recrimination and accusations of how this was all everyone else's fault. Old arguments, previously settled, usually with the blood of their rivals' followers, were brought up. All but one. Dionysus sat in the corner, drinking from his bottomless wine glass - he'd upgraded from the horn some time ago - glumly watching events unfold. He'd been 'invited' as an objective witness to events but failed to see what any of this had to do with him. He'd seen better days. Once he had been an athletic young man in the prime of his life. Now he had a beer belly. His hair, once a mass of shining gold curls, had receded to the back of his head and was now worn in a greying ponytail.

'Di,' Charon crouched next to him.

He nodded a greeting. 'Charon. Quite the to do you've started.'

'I didn't start it. This would have happened without my help.'

'Does telling yourself that help you sleep at night?' He lit a cigarette and took a deep drag.

'Not really. Look, I just passed on a message that Ra decided not to.'

'Fair enough. But have any of you in your 'infinite wisdom' stopped to consider the real reason why Ra didn't pass on that message, other than simply saving his own sorry skin, of course?'

Charon felt his face fall. He hadn't considered that Ra might be playing a bigger part than he'd made out. Now it all rushed through his head at once. He'd taken Ra's position to be mere cowardice rather than subterfuge. 'Do you think it's worth trying to tell this lot?'

'What do *you* think?' Dionysus scoffed and took another deep swig. Wine dribbled down his chin on to a crumpled white dress shirt that had already seen better days. The yellowing collar was open and a bow-tie hung over one shoulder. He hiccupped. 'This lot couldn't see past their own egos if their lives depended on it.'

'Their lives do depend on it. *All* our lives do.'

'There you go then.' He hiccupped again. 'Charon, you're a great guy, honest to a fault, but you're still underground where politics are concerned. This is the way of the world.' He waved his arm in the rough direction of the arguing deities and took another swig.

'That's rather cynical don't you think?!'

'Is it? Sorry.' Charon wasn't sure if he was being sarcastic, 'Change is scary, so they'll carry on doing what's been tried, even when it's failing in front of their eyes because it's familiar and safe. They'll claim they had to make 'tough choices' and that 'things have always been that way'. Even the mortals do it. For years and years, they complained that they didn't have the right leader, then one comes along that seems to finally fit the bill and the first thing they do is try to depose him. Undermined his supporters, slurred the names of party members, all in the name of getting 'the right man' in charge of the party.'

'If you're talking about what I think you are, didn't he win again with an even bigger majority? I have to admit that they have become incredibly creative about how they define democracy.'

'Creative is one word for it.'

'I know you don't see it, Di, but I just have to believe it's worth at least trying to be better than this lot. Otherwise what's the point?'

'There isn't one. Listen lad, I've been around a damned sight longer than you and one thing I can tell you is that things don't change. Time and events are circular. They mirror and overlap, humans act, and while details change two things are constant.'

'And they are?'

'Fear and greed. What else, boy? Sometimes it's weighted more heavily on one side than the other, but they are always there together.'

Charon just stared ahead. He couldn't bring himself to agree with all that Dionysus had said but he had a point. The gods were manifested from exaggerated human characteristics. He knew that, as much as any of the others, and no matter how much they liked to pretend they were above it, the gods were no different. Ra claimed he was acting out of fear, but what if it was greed? What did he stand to gain?

Charon stood 'Thanks, Di. You've been a great help.'

'Think nothing of it.'

As he left the still arguing gods, Charon felt his phone vibrate in his pocket. It was another text message, but instead of another warning to stay away, this time it was a time and date, and an address.

A. H. Johnstone

CHAPTER 19

The Whispers in the Dark

The night was bitterly cold and Charon wished dearly that he had worn a thicker jacket. A week had passed since that meeting and, so far, all had been quiet. If he had been able to get hold of Hermes he might have been able to snag a lift, but they had been ordered to stay away from each other. He checked his watch. Two in the morning. He was going to be late. He had been racking his brains all afternoon over what he could have been tipped off about. Would he finally be able to confront the clown who had been messaging him and tell them politely, but very firmly, to bugger off? Unlikely, but he had been given this information for a reason and it didn't look like the Olympians were prepared to put their differences aside for long enough to see off this crisis.

As he rounded a corner into an alley way he heard two voices whispering heatedly in the darkness. He stopped and crouched against the wall behind one of the big green wheelie bins. Thanks to the council's two-week rubbish collection, it stank. Listening carefully, he thought that one of the voices was familiar. Very familiar.

'I don't care what you have to do, get him off the case! You said reporting him would get his nose out of this!'

'I thought it would. I underestimated him. How was I to know he'd finally grow a spine?' the familiar voice whined.

'He's *your* friend.'

This statement piqued Charon's curiosity enough to peer over the top of the bin. Two figures stood opposite one another under the flickering orange light of a graffiti covered street lamp. He couldn't see their faces, but he had a sneaking suspicion that one of them was Hermes. He needed to be certain. Looking around on the ground at his feet, he found an old baked bean tin which hadn't quite met its target and threw it down the alley way. It clattered against a bin a few feet away from them. A terrified cat yowled and sped off into the night. The pair stopped talking and turned in his direction.

Charon felt sick. It was Hermes. He didn't recognise the other one.

'Hmm, just a cat,' said the taller one.

'Now he's played the hero and had a taste of being sent on a fruitless mission he should be happy enough to go—'

'You think so? We have no idea what went on in that forest, and now the dragon is dead we have no way to find out. I have a lot riding on this. If I fail, you fail with me. Odin and his bearded idiots will flay me if I am caught.'

'I didn't tip him off, Loki. Charon's having some sort of crisis. Thinks he can play the hero.'

'I know that. Odin only went to Ra because he didn't know how to contact Zeus but if it hadn't been for Ra's clumsy taste for the dramatic, nobody would have been any the wiser. All he had to do was not say anything. But oh no, call a meeting and draw attention to us, then your friend had to eavesdrop and come over all noble.'

'What do you want me to do about it?'

'Find out what he knows, get rid of him, and report back. I'll be in contact in two days to hand over Idunn's apples. They'll need to be delivered straight to Ra. I'll tell you where to leave them. I can't get away easily right now. Odin is watching me. He's always watching me.' He spat, wiped his mouth and carried on.

'Do I want to know what is special about these apples?'

'Idunn was able to sneak through a cutting from her tree in the crossing. It's taken her years to finally get it bearing fruit that can replenish the powers of the Aesir. There's not enough magic here. Who knows if there will be another crop. Ra wants them for himself.'

'Why?'

'Seriously? Do you not read? The apples are the secret to the Aesir's strength and vitality. Ra wants them to boost his own power. Plus, it will mean the Aesir won't have them when the time comes. Ra will be able to boost his power while the Titans and Giants deal with his enemies and rivals for him. He won't even have to use his own power to flood Midgard.'

'Midgard?'

'Here! This godsawful place of decay, no magic, and no end. Hel's domain is quite homely by comparison if you ask me. I just want to go home. So do you.'

'But do we have to—'

'This is the price which must be paid. See to it.' Loki turned and walked away. Once Charon was certain he had gone, he emerged from his hiding place.

'Charon! What are you doing here?'

Charon's face barely moved. His 'friend' was going to pretend he was just passing through. *Very well,* he thought. *Two can play that game.* Rage was building. He needed to find out how much Hermes knew. *How deep had the rot set in?*

'Just out for a walk. Thought it might clear my head. Jet lag you know.' He paused, 'why not come back to mine tonight? I have something I need to speak to you about.'

'Your sofa again? I won't be able to move in the morning but why not. How was the trip?'

'Enlightening.'

CHAPTER 20

The Enemy Bares its Teeth

The kitchen light flickered and buzzed after Charon hit the switch and put the kettle on. His head was reeling and he'd hardly said a word on the way home. Where should he start? He could hardly begin with, *'Hey, Hermes, when were you thinking about telling me that you and Loki were behind this whole mess?'* He would have to be subtle.

'Coffee?'

'Yeah, go on.' Hermes flopped down in one of the kitchen chairs and yawned.

'You okay?'

'Just dandy. Why?'

'I just could have sworn I saw someone giving you a hard time. Did you know him?'

'Nothing to worry about. Just a low-life after my phone.'

It was a good thing Charon had his back to him. It meant he wouldn't have seen Charon's rage. *He thinks I'm an idiot.* Why hadn't he seen this sooner? Thinking back, Hermes had done nothing but discourage him from following his conscience since this whole thing started. He had taken the look on his face when they had gone to spy on that meeting for fear. What he hadn't considered was why he might have been afraid.

Charon sat on the opposite side of the table and kicked off his walking boots. 'Really? He was talking like he knew you... Like he was blackmailing you.'

Hermes' face fell. 'What are you accusing me of?' He stood up and paced.

'Nothing at all.' Charon said. He didn't need to, Hermes' face told him everything he needed to know. 'But this is not the usual reaction to someone asking about your wellbeing.'

Hermes stopped pacing. 'You wouldn't understand.' He whispered.

'Try me.'

'Where would I start?' Hermes raked his fingers through his hair and scrubbed at his face.

'So, there is more to it?'

'I can only tell you my part. You have to promise that it will go no further.' Hermes continued to pace up and down the kitchen.

'We'll see. I can keep your name out of it, but if it's something we need to deal with, we're going to have to tell the right people. You can start by telling me who you were talking to.'

Hermes punched a wall in frustration, 'Loki.'

Charon almost choked on his coffee. '*The* Loki!?'

'The one and only. And he's every bit as slippery as his reputation would have him out to be. He makes promises and tells you what you want to hear and then once you have done as he asks, he has you.'

'Hermes, what did you do?'

'You don't understand. He promised me he could help us get home. We can go back to our own lives.'

'What did you do?'

'It was me. I let the Titans out. I... I was sick of being my father's flunky and I wanted my power back. I was going to take us all home and leave Zeus and his squabbling siblings here to rot.'

'And now?'

'And now the Titans have no interest in helping us. They've cast their lot with Loki and the giants. Loki is working for someone else. I don't know who, or what he intends.'

'So, you not only released our deadliest—'

'Not ours, Zeus's—'

'You think it matters to them!?' Charon picked up his mug and hurled it past Hermes' head so it smashed against the wall where Hermes had punched it. China flew everywhere and the dregs of his coffee ran down the wall.

'What was that for?' Hermes whined. 'I'm a victim

of circumstance—'

'Stop lying! I heard you, Herm. I know exactly what Loki said. Did you agree to come with me so you could find out what I knew and then get rid of me for your new friend?'

'You could join us. I could give you a better job than ferry—'

'Do I look stupid? You have no clue what Loki has planned for you. No, this must go higher. If you cut ties with Loki, I will try to keep your name out of it…'

'And what? Have this hanging over me from both directions? No thanks! I made my choice, Charon, and I offered you a slice of the pie.' He smiled but it didn't reach his eyes. 'What did the dragon tell you?'

'How do you know about that?'

'Some of the Norns are on our side. They told us you'd been there but the dragon's magic meant they couldn't hear what was said. The other Norns, the ones who remain loyal to Odin well, they can be dealt with later. Are you going to cooperate?'

'No. I don't think so.'

'Then it looks like I will just have to dispose of you too.' He grabbed the cleaver from the magnet on the wall and moved in on Charon.

Charon leapt from his chair, lifted it, and hurled it at Hermes who dodged. There was only one way out of the kitchen and Hermes had moved between it and Charon. He grabbed the handle of a small wooden chopping board and swung it at Hermes, knocking the knife out of his hand and allowing himself time to slip past Hermes while he scrabbled on the floor for the knife. The board hadn't been the most elegant of weapons but it had done the trick. Trouble was, Hermes was coming in for round two, and Charon had now disarmed himself.

He ducked into the hall cupboard and held the handle closed from the inside. Looking for something to defend himself with, he tried to calm himself as he heard Hermes creeping up the stairs. The iron was no good. It was heavy but he would have to get close to the swinging cleaver to use it with any effect and throwing it would be ineffective. It wasn't exactly aerodynamic. He fumbled around in the dark and came across something hard and angular and attached to a long metal pole. Then he remembered.

It was one of the set of golf clubs Hel had bought him as an anniversary present. He can't have taken them out more than three times since he'd owned them and Hel had threatened to sell them, and him with them, if he didn't start using them. Never had he been happier to find them than now. He felt for the sand wedge. It had a nice sharp edge and would deal a blow heavy enough to knock Hermes out. He hoped.

Quietly as he could, Charon opened the cupboard and slipped back into the living room. Hermes would soon figure out that he hadn't gone upstairs and come back to look for him. Walking backwards, he tried to figure out the best place to defend from but didn't see his 'cat' curled up on the floor and trod on its tail. It woke with a scream, swiped its claws down Charon's leg and sank its teeth into his ankle. The yell must've been heard from upstairs as Hermes came thundering back down, cleaver in hand, and a glazed look in his eyes.

Hiding around the corner so he couldn't be seen from the stairs, Charon took his chance and swung the club as Hermes crept past. It struck Hermes on the back of the neck, hard enough to daze but not render him unconscious. He had to hand it to the manufacturers, they were tough clubs.

Hermes pulled himself to a crawling position and felt the back of his neck. There was no blood but that blow would leave a nasty bruise. Charon tried to circle round him, leaping over the sofa, and hurling everything he could at his former friend.

Hermes managed to get to his feet despite this effort and gauged Charon's attempt to get past him, hurling the cleaver which sliced his arm as it sailed past. Charon aimed another swing at Hermes. As if in answer, Hermes grabbed the TV from its wall mount, yanked the cable from the wall and threw it at Charon, hitting him squarely in the chest and knocking him backwards into the wall. He felt something warm and sticky trickle down the back of his head as he slid down the wall, hugging the TV. Hermes stood over him with the cleaver.

'You could have joined us, you know. Claimed a nice cushy spot on Olympus. But you had to be difficult—'

'Don't give me that, Hermes. If I hadn't found out what I know now, you'd have let me drown with everyone else. You offered me a spot on 'the team' to ease your guilt.'

'Far too clever for your own good. My father and uncles really should have made better use of you. I can't back out now. I have too much to lose. You, however, had everything to gain and still threw it away. Oh well, too late now.' Hermes leaned over him and lifted Charon's chin with the blade.

'It's called integrity, Hermes. Maybe you should look it up? You start by not selling your people to weasels like Loki.' Charon's head spun.

Hermes laughed. 'I'll be certain to pass that message along. Were you not listening? Loki is working for someone else.'

'Heard.' He didn't need to think too hard about who. Who else but Ra? 'Don't care. If you're going to kill me Hermes, just get on with it. Only dodgy villains in bad films stand around gloating about it.' Charon felt the golf club under his legs which were now pinned by the TV. He shoved it off his lap and grasped the handle. Unfortunately, Hermes saw this and stepped on the handle, trapping Charon's fingers.

Hermes leaned down and began to prise it out of his grasp and Charon saw his chance. In one movement, he swung his free fist into the side of Hermes' head and his right knee up into his throat. Hermes toppled to the floor making gagging noises and clutching at his neck, and Charon, ignoring the deep gash across his arm, struggled to his feet, taking the club and the cleaver with him. The knock on his head was making him feel sick and dizzy. Looking down at his former friend he wondered what to do with him. No one would blame him for eliminating a threat in his own home but there was one important difference between him and them; he would not kill another to save his own skin. Hermes had been willing to drown billions just to see home again.

He pulled out his phone and called Zeus. This had to go higher and he would not hesitate to drop Hermes right in the cacky! Then it went black.

CHAPTER 21

The Tea Leaves

Charon wasn't sure who had called the ambulance, but nor did he much care. It couldn't have been Zeus as his call had not connected. He had left an angry message, demanding that Zeus call him back, dropping the phone on to the floor just as it screeched to a halt outside his house, sirens blaring. Looking down, he noticed blood on the screen. Was that his? The noise stopped but he could make out the flicker of lights reflected on what was left of the paint round the door. Hermes had left it open when he fled. The back of his head throbbed and he felt sick. What had Hermes hit him with? Whatever it was, he had lost nearly forty minutes. There was no way he could make chase now.

As he tried to pull himself off the floor to the sofa two paramedics rushed in with oxygen and a pack of supplies. He tried to wave them away but a familiar voice cut into their questions.

'Now, Mr Charon, if I am not mistaken you are quite as stubborn as your friend.'

'You?' It sounded like the nurse from the other evening, but he couldn't tell.

'Me, what? Just you listen to what these good people are saying and let them do their job. I will put the kettle on for some sweet tea. Lord knows, you look like you could do with a cup. I know I could.'

Charon pointed vaguely at the kitchen and the blurred shape of the nurse moved away. What was going on? The paramedics were busily checking his responses and asking him questions about who and where he was. Did they know *what* he was? This wasn't the first time he'd been injured. The last time he'd been hurt like this was during the eighth century. Waking up in a monastery which had just been raided by Vikings had not been a pleasant experience. Then there was the whole thing with the Inquisition. He shuddered. What would they do to someone like him now? He knew why the Fae were so antsy about being 'discovered'. *If the mortals found out they had gods living among them, what would they do?*

The nurse came back carrying a tray holding four mugs of steaming hot tea. This was an achievement on its own as he didn't recall owning a tea tray, least of all one covered in pink peonies. He certainly didn't remember owning the matching mugs. The paramedics, who had now finished their checks, took the tea and issued thanks to the nurse as they made their way back outside.

'I'm right here. You can tell me what's wrong.'

'Indeed, you are but that can wait for the moment. You and I need to have a little chat, Mr Charon.'

'We do?'

'We do.' Her voice was warm but firm. She clearly felt she knew something he didn't. 'Don't worry about them. They don't ask questions or spread little stories either.' She sat down beside him and settled the tray between them on the sofa.

'Fine. I don't suppose your bag of tricks holds something strong enough to make my head less painful? Elephant tranquilisers, for instance.'

She laughed 'That can wait. I need you clear headed for this. And drink your tea.'

'Why, what's in it?'

'Milk and sugar. What else?'

'Forgive me, but last time I came across humans who knew what I was, it didn't end well.' He took a sip. It was remarkably good considering the only milk he had was probably on the turn. There was something very odd about her.

'Your caution is wise. Now. Down to business. When was the last time you saw Robin Goodfellow?'

'That snot-nosed barman?' About a week ago. Why?'

'He was found this morning. Decapitated.' The blandness of her tone shocked him more than what she had said. It was so matter-of-fact. As if this was just one of those things that comes up in polite conversation.

'He what!'

'He was found behind the pub he worked at. The owner found him. Head four foot from his body. Blood everywhere...'

'Yes, yes, I don't need all the gory details. What does this have to do with me?'

'You were seen on a security tape having an, shall we say, 'animated' discussion with the deceased.'

'Ah.' Charon saw the point. 'In case you didn't notice, it wasn't me, having the 'animated discussion'. Hermes was the one giving him grief. I was trying to break up the fight.'

'I'm not interested in that right now. My point is that there was no sound on the tape and I need to know what Robin said.'

'Why?' Charon asked. Not out of concern for himself, but for Robin. Duplicitous little twerp that he was, nobody deserved to die like that.

'Because, Charon, what he said to you two is probably what got him killed. The Fae--'

'They exiled him. Why do they care?' Charon growled. 'They were the reason Robin turned spy.

One too many practical jokes and you're out. No wonder he was angry. They'd liked practical jokes well enough when the joke was not on them.'

'The Fae care very much. Even those they have exiled come under some sort of protection. He was still one of them and they are livid. Never seen them so angry. Or so worried. They reckon your sniffing around and interference is what caused it and will not hesitate to make you pay.'

'Just you hang on a bloody minute! Let me get this straight. *None* of this was my idea. I found out something... something big. I did my bit. I passed on the message. I haven't told the Council which, by the way, is probably going to end up getting me into even more trouble when I get found out. I've been sent here, there and bloody everywhere as some sort of messenger. I discovered that my best mate not only tried to land me in it, but is in this up to his eyebrows, and now *I* am on the hook for the death of an exiled faery who wouldn't be dead had the Fae bothered to get their hands dirty and stop something before it started. They knew what was going on. They just didn't want to get involved.'

'That's pretty much it, yes.'

Charon sighed and scrubbed his face with his hands. 'Hermes just went mad… dragged him—'

'I know that. What did he *say*?'

'Something about the giants planning to betray the Titans… Look I'm not sure I should be telling you this. How do I know you didn't have something to do with it?'

'Short answer? You don't.'

'So why should I tell you anything?'

'Good point but let me ask you a question. Why, if I wanted to harm you, would I have just helped you?'

'You sent the ambulance? How did you even--'

'That doesn't matter. I am not your enemy,' the Nurse said. 'I need to know. If the Fae catch up with you, before I can fill them in on a few things, a bump on the noggin will be the least of your worries.'

'Oh yeah? And what happens if whoever deprived Robin of his 'noggin' comes looking for me because I spoke to you?' Charon ground his teeth and found himself gripping his mug so tightly it might break. He loosened his grip.

'Another good question, but not one I can answer. At least not now. Now is not the time for that. You have caused quite the stir. Your display with Zoë was not the least of the troubles I have had to tidy up.'

'You knew about that? I thought Wadjet…?

'You think a goddess of her standing can't delegate?' She sighed, 'Look. It's complicated. Put simply, I'm neither one of you, nor one of 'us'.'

'Some might say you're both.'

'Hmm, that's nice of you, but it puts me at the bottom of a very long pecking list.'

'Trust me, I know the feeling.' Charon grumbled. *What choice do I have?* 'Fine.'

'Good? You were saying about the Giants and the Titans?'

'That's all he said. Oh, and he hinted that Hermes couldn't be trusted, which to be fair, turned out to be true.'

'Really? In what sense?'

'In the sense that *he* released the Titans, tried to recruit me, and when I turned his offer down, he tried to take my head off. If you ask me, there's your suspect.'

'That would certainly seem to be the case.' She swirled her cup, considered the bottom, and paused. She shook her head and put the cup down on the tray, took Charon's from him, and did the same. After a few moments of silence, she put the other cup back on the tray. 'Both interesting and unfortunate.'

'What do you mean?'

'We are at a crossroads, Charon. These events are very rare but they do happen and this time they appear to centre on you.'

'What! Why?'

'The why is not important. What matters is the what for? I cannot say what you must do because both outcomes will have dire consequences. It is not my place to influence you.' She stood up to leave.

Out of habit, Charon stood too.

'And they are? Or can't you tell me that either?'

'Mr Charon, while you have things you cannot tell me...'

The room went cold. This had gone far enough and Charon was sick of the secrecy. 'Tell me!' He hadn't meant to do 'the voice' and the glowing eyes, but the woman was trying his patience. He had a job to do and she was not helping. 'Sorry, but you have questioned me. Now I need information from you.'

'Oh, very well, but I don't take kindly to being spoken to like that,' she snapped. 'The first possible outcome is not a happy one. If the gods cannot set aside their differences and mistrust, the titans and the giants will rid themselves of their ancient enemies, but then turn on each other. There will be no Ragnarök. No renewal. They will consume the earth and everything in it.'

That would put a crimp in Ra's plans, thought Charon, but it would explain Zoë's reaction. The poor girl had all that in her head? No wonder she was terrified. Charon cleared his throat 'And the second?'

'This is not so certain. It shows a battle and a victory, but not a final one. It is not Ragnarök, though many will believe it is. The rest is not clear. There will be blood and loss in both cases, Charon, and I fear you have yet more to lose.'

A. H. Johnstone

CHAPTER 22

The Unexpected Guest

Shortly after the nurse had left there was a knock at the door. Charon didn't answer. Maybe if he ignored them, they would take a hint. He wasn't in the mood for any more guests. Whatever it was could wait until he'd had some sleep. There it was again, but more persistently this time. *Go away,* he thought. He just wanted some peace and quiet. Was that too much to ask? Clearly it was. The persistent knocking turned into a very adamant pounding which was rattling the windows either side, and Charon suspected that ignoring it any more would result in a lack of front door. Whoever it was pounded again.

'Alright! I'm coming! Do you know what bloody time it is? Some of us need to work in the—' He opened the door to be met by the jovial face of Erick.

In full battle dress.

'Odin wants to see you. I was told to bring you directly.'

'What, now?'

'No, next week. Yes *now*!'

Charon sighed. 'Fine. You'd better come in.' He stalked back into the house to find his keys and coat.

Erick followed him and let out a long, low whistle. 'What happened here?'

'Hermes happened.' Charon had found his coat and was in the process of patting down pockets in search of his phone and keys. He found his phone on the floor where the paramedics had treated his cuts and bumps. It was smeared with blood and the screen was scratched but it worked. The bowl he normally kept his keys in was in pieces on the floor but he couldn't see where they had landed. He knelt to peer under the side table. They were at the back.

'Hermes? The guy who was with you the other night?' Erick leaned on his axe.

'That's him.' Charon reached behind the unit, trying to hook his keys with a wire coat hanger.

'I thought you two were friends.'

'So…ah, bugger!' A metallic jingle signalled that they had slipped further out of reach 'So did I, up until tonight. As it turns out, I am not such a good judge of character. I probably should have seen it coming. Once a trickster, always a trickster, and the thing about Hermes… is that he has… always acted out of calculated self-interest.'

'I was sent to find you as you had vanished. Odin was worried. It seems that events have moved on.'

'Yes – Ah ha!' He stood up, keys in hand. 'That's certainly one way of putting it. Another way would be to say that Hermes has dropped us all in the midden.'

'Well, whatever it is, it must be serious. Your eyes are doing that blue glowy thing.'

'It's a long story. I'll explain on the way. Let's get moving.'

* * *

It hadn't taken long to get there, thanks largely to Erick's motorbike and sidecar. What he hadn't expected was the colour. Canary yellow wasn't on the top of the list of colours that Charon understood to be 'unlikely to draw undue attention' but at three o'clock in the morning, very few people were likely to notice them. He'd been handed a battered old helm with a nose piece. Charon had to ride pillion because the sidecar was currently occupied by more weapons than two people could possibly need.

As they pulled up outside the old factory, Odin was waiting for them, grim faced, and with a full retinue of guards behind him. His one blue eye bore into Charon. 'You took your time.'

So much for a keeping a low profile, Charon thought. What he said was 'Yes, well. If you'll give me a moment to recover from Erick's driving, I'll explain.'

'You'll speak to me with some respect—'

'I'm not here through my own volition. You summoned me, remember? So you'll listen to what I have to say. This will take a while so I suggest we go inside.'

It took about an hour to explain what had happened since their last meeting. He described the encounter with Zoë. He told him that Zeus had tried to cover his own tracks with the Council just to hold on to his position. He told them what the Dragon had said about Zeus being unable to defeat the Titans alone which is why they had been imprisoned. He told them about the meeting when he returned which had descended into chaos.

'Is that all?' Odin asked.

'All? I don't think there is an 'all' that I could possibly explain. But no. That is not 'all'. I thought it was until tonight. There is no easy way to say this but Hermes was working under Loki. He let the Ice Giants out and convinced Hermes that if he got the Titans out and on side, there would be a golden handshake in there for him.'

'But why would Loki do this?' Odin asked, confused.

'Why do you think? He wants to go home and he thinks that this is the way to do it. What he doesn't realise is that the Ice Giants have no intention of playing by his rules.' Charon said. He wondered if they knew about Robin Goodfellow. Never mind... he'd chance it if only to see the look on their faces.

'What you mean 'play by his rules'?' A voice from the crowd piped up. He couldn't be sure but the voice sounded female.

'Based on what Robin told us the other night, the Giants intend to not only betray the Titans, but the people who let them out too.' He followed this with an unspoken statement, *but what I hadn't taken on board at the time were Robin's hints that Hermes was involved.* Should he tell them what the Nurse said too?

'Did Robin actually say that Loki was involved?' Odin asked suspiciously.

'No.' *Now is the time.* Taking a deep breath, he stilled himself for the onslaught of questions that would follow. 'But what Robin knew lost him his head!' *Dead Fae can spill no secrets.* 'There is also the little fact that I saw Loki and Hermes discussing what they have done in an alley not four hours ago. When I confronted Hermes and refused to join him he tried to kill me.'

The crowd gasped and Charon heard whispering. *They don't believe me. They think this is going to go away if they ignore it for long enough.* As the attention was no longer on him, Charon stood and walked towards the fire for extra warmth. He couldn't leave now. Not until he had convinced them that the danger was real. Charon knew that Odin didn't trust him. Not fully. Even though it had been Odin who had warned him of the danger and asked his employee to visit Zeus and tell him what was going on. *What is it about gods that makes them incapable of trusting any judgement but their own?* For centuries, even before they were thrown from their own worlds by Yahweh, they had been beset by infighting and squabbles. The fighting and feuding had been replaced by a sullen silence between all of them, but nothing had ever been resolved. The old animosity had been shut away and locked up, waiting for an opportunity to burst out. And here it was, under their very noses and orchestrated by two minor deities who were so sick of the restrictions placed upon them by life in the mortal world that they were willing to destroy everything just to go home.

'How do we know that you refused to join Hermes?' Odin asked. 'We have only your word and you are not one of us. Hermes is your friend, so why would you turn from him?'

'Because I am not psychotic, that's why!' Charon snapped. He calmed himself. 'I know what the Titans are capable of. I wouldn't trust them to hold up their end of a bargain with a God any more than I would trust Zeus's final words.' The Norse were old but they had not been there when Zeus and Poseidon had been unable to defeat them so incarcerated them instead. Why would they be? They had their own troubles with the Ice Giants at the time. It was also unlikely that either the Giants or the Titans would willingly go back into their boxes and play nicely. 'I know better than to trust any of them,' Charon said, calmer now. 'I should have known better than to put Hermes' persuasion to stay out of it down to concern for my well-being. That is my mistake and something I will have to live with. Whatever Hermes was, he was not my friend.'

'That is maybe,' Odin said, 'but your loyalties must

be with your own people. You are Greek. Whatever your connection to us in the past, that fact remains.'

'Ahh,' Charon said, 'so this goes back to Hel, does it?' He should have known this would come up. 'May I remind you that it is she who left me? And before you ask, no, I do not know where she is.'

'I do not think you can be entirely objective in this instance. After deep consideration, I think I had better approach Zeus myself. I trust you can arrange this Charon. Again, I would like to keep the Council out of this.'

'I did what you asked of me,' Charon said quietly.

'Granted, but you are not one of us—'

'Hel was my wife!'

'Yes, and the two of you married in secret, against the express wishes of both of your peoples! You nearly started a war!' Odin bellowed, and slammed his fists down on the table in front of him. 'That, Mr Charon, is why we cannot trust you.'

'There is no law against what we did!' Charon felt his heart race with hurt and rage. The pain of her absence was as fresh as it had ever been. Tears burned behind his eyes. How dare they use Hel against him? They had found love. They had been happy. Then, she was gone, and he was left alone again. *But now is not the time for this.* He had to remain focused but, if he got through this alive, he would find Hel and win her back.

'That doesn't make it right!'

'Really? Who were we hurting?'

'It's not about who you were hurting. You defied your leaders. Both of you.'

'I defied orders so I could pass on your message too. Or is it a different matter when it works in your favour, Odin? From where I stand you are as much a hypocrite as Zeus!'

'Charon, that's enough! Now is not the time.' A female voice rang behind him. It was familiar. Kind, but with all of Odin's command. It couldn't be…

Charon turned slowly and faced her. His knees buckled in shock and relief, and he was suddenly on the ground. She was here. 'You…' That was it. She was okay. His tears flowed, and he wrapped his arms around her waist, buried his face in her and begged the world for this to be real.

A. H. Johnstone

CHAPTER 23

The Ex-Wife!

'Charon? Charon. Stand up.' One desiccated hand lay on his shoulder as the other, healthy and manicured, stroked his greying hair. She whispered to him, 'Charon, I know this is a terrible shock, but you need to get up now.'

'Why?'

'Why what?'

'Why anything?'

'You are still needed. You must speak to Zeus again. We must stop this.'

Charon looked up, seeing his wife's face for the first time in decades. She was as impressive as ever. 'I'll give you his number. He doesn't trust me either. You'll be in good company.'

'Charon...'

Shock gave way to anger, 'You left me! I heard nothing for thirty years and here you are. Under my nose. I thought you had faded. I grieved for you! For years!' He stood and brushed the dust from his trousers. 'And you were here all along! Had a good laugh at me have you everyone? Stupid old Charon. Always trusting. Let's play a good joke.'

'It wasn't like that at all. How long since you have slept?'

'I'm not a child who can be sent to bed when they get tiresome!'

'No, you aren't, but you have not rested in weeks, not properly. You will need your strength in the next few days. Erick! Take him to my rooms and see he sleeps. Knock him out if you have to.'

Erick obliged.

* * *

A few hours later Charon woke. After detangling

himself from an impractical number of furs and sheepskins on Hel's bed, he decided to apologise to Odin for his display. He'd had a point. No one in this situation had been entirely blameless. If the Council found out, they would all be in deep trouble but if he hadn't been sneaking around, he wouldn't have known about the meeting, or what was going to happen. Then again, nor would they, and none of them would have found out about Hermes and Loki until it was too late. He still had to wonder who had tipped him off about Loki and Hermes. Robin had been found that morning, so it could not have been him.

As he left the room, he realised that he had no idea where in the building he was. There were no windows, so he had to be somewhere in the middle. He slid the door open as quietly as possible. Thankfully, the rails had been oiled. On the wall opposite Hel's room was a peeling sign pointing people to the fire exit at the end of the corridor. Charon decided that the best bet for finding Odin would be to go the other way. Following the noise of snoring and some horribly organic smells, Charon came to a door he recognised. He stopped. The door was ajar and he heard a heated discussion which seemed to be about him.

'I told you to stay in the back and out of sight!'

'Yes. But you also promised not to use me against him. You broke your word.'

'That's irrelevant!'

'Is it? You cast doubt on *his* reliability while ignoring your own promises?'

'No... it's not like that at all.'

'So, is trust only one sided? I will not tell others you broke your word to me, Odin, but I will not hesitate to remind you. Charon was... is correct. The rules only appear to apply when they are in favour of you gods. Liars and thieves are the masters of self-justification, aren't they? Charon and I are not gods. Nor is my father. Are we forever to be considered expendable?'

Odin eyed her. He knew better than to cross Hel. She was correct about not being a god. Technically, like her father, Loki, she was a giantess and she had a *very* long memory. She had not forgotten what they had done to her brother, Fenrir, just because they feared him. She had been banished to Nilfheim to care for the souls of those who had died of age or sickness because they could not allow her to roam freely. It had been under the pretext of giving her responsibility, but Odin suspected that she knew the truth. It was a means by which to contain her. They had done to Hel and the Giants, what Zeus had done to the Titans. 'Yes, I was getting to the point of your father. Where does your loyalty lie, girl?'

'My loyalty lies in its proper place, sire.'

'Obscure as ever, Hel. You have a place in the final battle. I cannot interfere with that course of events. But the same cannot be said about your husband. He has outlived his usefulness. Once he has delivered his message to Zeus--'

'You would kill him? He has done no harm to us.' Her voice was flat, but her eyes spoke her rage.

Odin had to bring her around. Then she would be free to marry someone who would bring him an advantage.

'Has he not?'

'No. He has not! As well you know.'

'He is not one of us. Our laws do not protect him.'

'That record is getting old, Odin. They may not protect him, but they bind *our* actions.' She folded her arms and pursed her lips. 'It would appear that our laws only apply when it works in your favour. My word, isn't that convenient.'

'Your judgement on the matter was not invited, girl!' he bellowed, 'Had you not become involved with him in the first place, I would have no decision to make!'

'So, you would have simply murdered him? You hypocrite! You speak so highly of honour, and valour in combat but when it comes to it, you're as cowardly as any mortal.'

He blanched at those words, and momentarily raised a hand in anger. 'Not all things are as simple as you would like them to be, my girl.' He threw the last of the contents of his horn into the fire pit, 'You are Loki's daughter. That makes you practically my granddaughter... you are family but you are not my conscience.'

'There is no need to make excuses. I know that if I were not Loki's child, or if you did not love my father as a son, you would have slaughtered me where I stood when you found me. Your loyalty to me, lies only in your love for my father, but what now Odin? My father has betrayed you, yet here I am, showing you the loyalty you withhold from all others. All I ask is for you not to harm Charon.'

'He is a spy!'

'He is no such thing! Even if he is, it is what you have made of him!' She stood almost nose to nose with him, her voice raised every bit as high as Odin's. 'He did what you asked, and passed your message on to Zeus?'

'And what else has he passed on to Zeus? Our numbers? Our weaknesses? Has he told the council about our business?' He gripped the top of Hel's healthy arm, but she pulled away in disgust.

'Gah! You're paranoid! I cannot speak to you when you are like this.' She stormed out.

Charon saw her coming and ducked into a shadow as she came into the corridor, shouting obscenities about gods and their 'promises'. He held his breath until she had passed, hoping that she wouldn't be checking on him. He needed his absence to remain unnoticed. Charon had heard enough. Hel had tried, and by god he still loved her fire, but Odin was dead-set on disposing of him once he delivered his message. He should have suspected this. Gods! It doesn't matter which pantheon they come from, when it boiled down to it, most of them were self-serving bastards. He should have known that Odin would have some plan up his sleeve. Well, he couldn't stay here. There was only one thing he could do. Charon ran.

* * *

A door in the distance slammed, making Odin start. 'What was that? I gave no one authorisation to leave!'

'It was probably just the wind, sir,' Erick said, yawning. He did not want to go out in the cold. The sun was up now, but the air was still freezing. 'It was probably Hel getting some air.'

'Go and find out! And wake our guest. He has a job to do.'

'Sir?'

'What is it?'

'Are you really going to kill him? He seems harmless enough.'

'With any luck, I won't have to. The final battle is coming. It may solve that little problem for me. Something Charon said earlier got me worried. If the Council do find out about any of this it won't just be his neck on the line for not raising the issue. It'll be mine too. Just go and see what that noise was.'

'And Loki?'

'Loki will be dealt with. Go!'

A. H. Johnstone

CHAPTER 24

The Passing of the Torch

It didn't take Erick long to find Charon. He sat at a bus stop, coat wrapped tightly around him and teeth chattering.

'You'll be waiting a while,' he said, tossing the motorcycle helmet to him. 'This bus route no longer runs.'

'Thanks. Can't say I'm surprised.' He shivered. 'I just want to go home, but Odin knows where that is.'

'You heard all that huh?'

'I think people in Belgium heard that.' Charon said grumpily, 'Call me old fashioned, but last time I checked, plotting to murder someone generally requires stealth and secrecy. Shouting so loud that your victim can hear you on the other side of a factory, could possibly be considered boastful.'

'Yes, but you can't tell gods anything.' Silence passed slowly. 'So, where would you like me to take you?'

'Won't you get into trouble?'

'Yes, but Odin's plan doesn't sit well with me. I did not get into Valhalla by being a sneak and a cheat.' He smiled. 'You have a lot to learn about Vikings.'

'What does it matter? Both sides want to kill me. Whatever I do now, I'm dead.'

'What about Zeus?'

'What about him?'

'He doesn't want you dead.'

'Yet. If I had just told the council...'

'If you had we would be in a worse position. They are supposed to be all-knowing, so, where are they? Sitting back and watching, no doubt. This is the first interesting thing that has happened in a millennium, unless you count the renaissance. But that was just funny.'

'The Renaissance?'

'All those paintings of faeries and goddesses in the altogether, and mythological scenes?'

'What about them?'

'Let's just say that not all of them were from the imagination, and not all the models were human.'

'Oh!' He smiled. Charon vaguely remembered censorship boards being set up, but he had thought that had been down to the church. If the council had been in on it too... well, it would have kept them busy. He imagined the council scurrying all over sixteenth century Europe trying to keep their world a secret and giving wayward dryads a slap on the wrist.

'Icarus was one of the worst. Biggest poser going.'

'I thought he...'

'Died? Yes, so did the rest of us. Turns out he faked his death to get away from dear old dad. Look, you know stories have power. They bring us to life and keep us going. I don't even think I was born. Not in the traditional sense. My first memory is fighting beside Beowulf, then I remember dying, so at best I was literary collateral damage. Does wonders for one's humility, I can tell you.'

'But what does this have to do with me?' Charon asked.

'My friend, if the story is written against you, what you need to do is—'

'Change the story?'

'I was thinking more like hunt down the author and gut him in front of his family, but your plan works too.'

'I think it would be less messy to go straight to Zeus. He's bound to have got my message by now.'

'So that's where we're going. Hop on, I'll give you a lift.'

* * *

They pulled up in front of the conference centre

that Charon had left a week earlier. It was dark, bar a single office on the second floor. He saw Zeus at the window clutching a steaming cup and looking harassed. The reason for this expression emerged a moment later in the form of Hera. By the look of things, she was tearing verbal strips off him. He felt sorry for Hera. She had been forced to endure his jibes and adultery for hundreds of years with no hope of finding her own relief - not that she hadn't caused her own fair share of trouble. Remember Troy? Then, to add insult to injury, she was forced to take a subordinate role in this world too. He truly hoped she would come out on top of it. It wasn't possible to make a bigger cods-up of it than her brother. At least, Charon didn't think so.

'They're upstairs.' Charon said.

'Maybe I had better wait out—'

'No.'

'No?'

'This affects us all. Plus, you can back me up. Zeus is every bit as cantankerous and mistrustful as Odin. Probably more so.'

'This isn't making me want to go up there any more than I did before.'

'Yes, well. Someone needs to give Odin the good news if Zeus decides to zap me.'

'Can he still...?'

'Up until this point, I have been lucky enough to never have reason to find out. I would like for it to stay that way.' Charon looked up at the window again. Zeus looked straight at him, tapping his watch impatiently. *Well, I guess that's my cue.*

They made their way upstairs after spending ten minutes arguing with the night doorman about following proper procedures, opening hours, and it not being like this in his day. Being on the other end of that sort of conversation was a little unnerving for Charon until he realised that he had witnessed a genius at work. It had it all: the delay tactics, the deliberate misinterpretation of procedure to defend laziness, and most of all the belligerent mistrust of all who tried to enter *his* building. After all, anyone turning up to a meeting more than forty minutes before normal opening hours *had* to be up to no good. If miracles happened, and he survived this unholy mess, he would have to start practicing.

'The office is over there.'

As if on cue, Hera marched out of the office. Her face was thunderous and seeing Erick did not improve matters. It occurred to Charon that, having learned of Hermes' treachery it might have been prudent to come here with the news first. Getting the news second hand would not improve his situation but at this point, he couldn't see any possible way for it to get worse.

'Charon, get in here! Do you think we have all day?'

'Erick has information too.'

'Really?' she sniffed, looking him up and down, then taking a deliberate step back, 'What information can he possibly have that would be of any use to us?'

'Odin plans to kill Charon.' Erick said, leaning on his axe.

'He what!'

'Look, I need to speak to Zeus and he's waiting.

I've already had to talk my way past the guy downstairs.' Charon didn't wait for permission. He and Erick marched into Zeus's office and stood in front of the desk.

Zeus looked like he hadn't slept for days. His previously pristine designer suit was crumpled, he had at least three day's growth on his chin, and his eyes were puffy and red.

'As much as I hate to make your day any worse than it already is, I have some bad news about your son.'

Zeus sat bolt upright and stared at Charon before pausing. 'Which one?'

'Hermes.'

'I told him to stay away from you. You were supposed to stay away from him! Does nobody do anything they're told anymore?'

'I *was* staying away. I got a text message as I left your last meeting. I say meeting. Utter bloody shambles is more like it.'

'And?'

'And I followed the instructions. It's a good thing I did, or I wouldn't be able to tell you what I know.'

He sighed and scrubbed his face with his hands, 'Sit. Both of you.' He pressed the intercom. 'Three more coffees please.'

'Charon, what has got into you? For years, you were a good employee. You did your job and didn't get involved in things that were not your concern. Now you're disobeying orders and mixing with...' He gestured at Erick.

'Vikings.' Erick volunteered. 'You'll find us quite friendly... most of us.' He raised his axe and leaned it on his shoulder.

'Thank you for that clarification. I take it there is a good reason there is a Viking in my office, Charon?'

'I'm getting to that. Let's just say I woke up and leave it at that.'

Hera entered with a catering trolley. It held the three coffees he asked for. It also held the biggest pile of bacon and cream cheese bagels Charon had ever seen. His mouth watered.

'I only asked for coffee…'

'The Sandwich Lady pulled up as I was on my way up so I bought the lot. You all need a proper breakfast. No arguments, brother. You look terrible.' She forced a bagel into his hand. 'Don't make me stay here and watch you eat that.'

'Fine. Are you planning to sit in?' he asked.

'If it pleases you. Let me just fetch my coffee before it gets cold.' Instead of leaving the room, she gave the trolley the merest glance and another cup of coffee appeared.

'Stop showing off, Hera.'

'Okay, sorry.' She sat down in a chair that Charon swore had not been there a moment ago and pulled out a notebook and a very expensive looking pen.

Charon looked over at Erick who was now staring at Hera, 'Stop staring, it just encourages them,' he whispered.

'Is she a witch?'

'Hera? Only in temper. She was Zeus' consort at

one time. A queen in all but title.'

'But she said 'brother'?'

'It was a different time... Best not to mention it.'

'Is she single now?'

'What! Possibly... Now is *not* the time!'

Erick grinned.

'When you two are quite finished whispering, we can begin,' Hera said. Her lips pursed but there was amusement in her eyes and Charon could have sworn that she winked at Erick.

'Thank you, Hera, but this is *my* office.'

'Don't be a child, Zeus. This is bigger than us. Just listen.'

'Fine, fine. Get on with it.' He pinched the bridge of his nose.

'Where was I?'

'You received a message from an unknown party and followed the instructions. Do you have a death wish?'

'Not that I know of, sir.' It didn't take long to explain all that had happened between bumping into Hermes and now. He'd hoped it would take longer. Somehow, ten minutes didn't do it justice. He'd decided to leave out what the nurse had told him but realised he couldn't articulate it even if he wanted to. The words stuck in his throat.

'Would I be correct to say that I am receiving this information second hand?' Zeus asked quietly.

Ever the arrogant fool. Just has to be the first in line for everything. 'Did you not hear me?' Charon asked. 'Your son is working with Loki. *He* released the Titans, and Odin plans to kill me, but you are worried about not having heard this first?'

'I heard you. Whatever my son has done is an internal matter and should have been treated with discretion. I now find out that you have been discussing our business with outsiders—'

'Zeus, stop. I can't listen to you blather on any longer. You know why he went to Odin first. He just told you. You look for fault in everything he does, but you are forgetting something vital, dear brother.'

'And that is?'

'That if you had not imprisoned the Titans simply for daring to be stronger than us, we would not be in this situation now. We drew first blood in the last war, and when we realised we would lose we locked our problems away and pretended they weren't there. The dragon told you at the time that you were building trouble for a later day. Well, here it is. At our doors. Charon has been doing your job for weeks because you would rather not dirty your hands with your own mess. Don't you dare try to deflect this on to him.'

'Hera--'

Before the conversation descended into a domestic incident, Erick stepped in with the message, 'Odin wants to meet with you to discuss how to deal with this. He too thinks Charon has done all he can for us. Unfortunately, he also wants Charon dead.'

'Why would he bother to kill Charon? He is no threat to him.'

'Odin disagrees. He knows where Odin's hall is. He knows our numbers. As far as Odin is concerned that makes him a threat. He also knows everything that has gone on over the last few weeks, including the failure to inform the council.'

'I see, but that puts us all in danger. Ra too. Everyone who was at that meeting is now at risk of losing their position. None of us questioned why they weren't at the meeting.'

'And that, I think, is what Ra is counting on. He is using your own lust for power against you.' said Charon

'Humph. Preposterous. None of them know that Charon had eavesdropped.'

'Possibly true. But you don't know that none of them called the Council as soon as they were out of earshot. They deal with their matters 'internally' too. For all we know they've been on to us since day one,' said Erick.

'You know an awful lot for a minor member of Odin's court.'

'I'm trusted with certain things, not all. I'm not technically supposed to be here, but Charon seemed to think he'd need me to back up his story. I can see why. You share much with Odin, not all of it is for the better.'

'Enough! I'll meet with Odin. When would he like to meet? I trust it will not be at his current hall?' Zeus said.

'Correct. He says the details are up to you.' said Charon.

'I will meet with him here, at sunset, two days from now. That should give me time to locate and question Hermes. I want to hear his side--'

Charon spluttered. 'His side? He told me what he did. He told me why. I told you everything he said and did. He betrayed us all and you want to see if my story measures up to scrutiny?' He shook his head. *Some people just don't change*.

'Don't you have a message to pass on?' Zeus sneered.

'Yes. If I survive, I'll give you a call,' said Charon.

A. H. Johnstone

CHAPTER 25

The Storm Builds

'What do you plan to do?' asked Erick, as they left the building.

'About?' Charon replied, his mind was not on the task of walking and he tripped over the low wall which ran around the forecourt and seemed to serve no other purpose than to mark a boundary line.

After much swearing about bloody stupid ornamental architecture being put right where people can walk into it and Erick helping him to his feet, Erick continued. 'Passing on that message. You can't exactly go wandering into Odin's hall again. Not when you know he plans to kill you.'

'I know that. Why do you think Zeus sent me? He wants rid of me too but if Odin does it he'll get to come over all indignant about Odin 'breaking the rules' and come out smelling of roses. I've served my purpose.'

'Well? How do you propose to get around that?'

'There isn't a way around it.'

'There is. Well there is if *you* aren't too proud to ask.'

'You'll be in enough trouble for helping me. I couldn't ask you to risk your life.'

'My life? I told you. I'm already dead. That is, I am if I was ever alive. The memory of that story is still so strong even minor players got a sort of half-life. It's really very confusing.' Erick mounted his bike and strapped his helmet on.

'How do you deal with it?'

'Mead. Stop changing the subject.' He passed Charon the helmet, 'You're clearly not going to ask so let me save your pride – you lot and your pride, geez: I thought we were bad – I will take the message to Odin. *You* think of somewhere to hide for the next two days that isn't home. Odin knows where you live and that's the first place he'll send someone to look.'

'Okay, take me— '

'Don't tell me! I can't know. I need to look him in the eye when I tell him I don't know where you are and I am not a good liar. I'll drop you home so you can collect some things, then I'll be on my way. I don't even want to tell him which direction you went.'

* * *

Two days later, Charon was waiting outside the conference centre again. To be strictly accurate, he was hiding behind one of the huge bushes by the entrance, watching people going in. He hadn't wanted to be the first one there just in case the next person to arrive happened to be somebody who wanted him dead. As plans went, it wasn't a bad one as nobody had seen him. Yet. Something had to go right for him, if only by the law of averages, and the last forty-eight hours had been utterly miserable. In the end, he'd been forced to hide at work and live off a cold Chinese takeaway. This had not been pleasant, and there seemed to have only been one dry area in the whole building. Then he had been caught trying to sneak out so that he could pretend to come back in. It certainly had been interesting trying to explain to the night watchmen why he was there and why there was a camp-bed and a sleeping bag in the boiler room. He was cold, hungry and very stiff, and something told him that the day was not going to improve.

Finally, the coast was clear. Charon slipped out from behind the bush and through the front doors. The front desk wasn't manned so he sneaked across the foyer and up the service stairs unseen. He hoped there was a service door into that room. If there wasn't he would have to double back and get past Hera and Hestia. He hadn't been expressly banned from the meeting, but nor had he been invited. He needed to know what was going on, and he was dead certain that Zeus wouldn't be sharing it. At least, not with him. If all went well, he'd be able to get in and out without being noticed.

Thankfully there *was* a service door and enough

people were crowded round it that he could creep in and stand at the back. How many people had Zeus called here? He clearly wanted to make an example of somebody. Could he have found Hermes? He wasn't there from what he could see, but that didn't mean he wasn't in the building. He concentrated on slowing his breathing, it wouldn't do to draw attention to himself by exposing his nervousness. He had to look like he was supposed to be there.

The main doors of the office opened and Odin marched in with a stream of attendants. At the rear were the two men who had driven the van that had taken him to Odin the other evening. They looked just as fearsome under proper light as they had under the streetlamps. They dragged a chained figure with a hessian bag over his head. It was filthy and stained with blood. The man's hands were bound behind him and he was so weak that he couldn't keep his balance. The men hauled him into the middle of the room and kicked him roughly to his knees. Would this be an execution? Charon hoped not. He'd seen enough of them in his long years, and some of the people delivered to him on the Styx had arrived in buckets. Well, bits of them had. He wasn't sure he had the stomach for this but he was here now.

'Well, Zeus, I have delivered my man. Where is yours?' Odin bellowed. Charon wondered if he was capable of doing anything quietly.

'My man has been apprehended. Though I must say, he is in a happier state than yours.

'Show me.'

'All in good time. Why the hurry, Odin? Keen to get back to the comfort of your hall while better men clear up your mess?'

'My mess?'

'Your man deceived Hermes. Loki tricked him into releasing our enemies and was fool enough to believe the Ice Giants could be controlled. Now we must contain the problem and put your toys back in their box too.'

'I assure you, were it that simple, I would be quite capable of packing away my own toys, as you put it. But I did not do this to Loki.'

'No?'

'No. That was our enemy. As you said, he was

fool enough to think he could lead them. Once your Titans entered the equation, and believe me they *are* working together for now, he was no longer of use to them. When he tried to enforce his authority, they beat him up and dumped him on my doorstep last night.'

'So why is he in chains?'

'I am no fool. He betrayed us. An example must be set.'

'I see.' Zeus leaned back in his chair and steepled his fingers.

'Where the situation becomes complicated is that punishing our miscreants will not solve the problem.'

'And just how do you expect us to solve our little problem, Odin? I have it on good authority that you plan to kill one of my people. I'm also tasked with investigating the death of a fae. One...' Zeus peered at a notebook by his elbow, 'Robin Goodfellow.'

A voice mumbled from under the bag. Odin signalled for it to be removed, and the two men dragged it roughly from his head. Loki had been gagged as well, 'Ha 'as a f'ilt'y 'by.' he mumbled.

Odin pulled the gag down, 'What? You have more to say? My, my, aren't we talkative today. Speak your piece.'

Loki coughed, 'I said, he was a filthy spy! I had no choice.'

'So unusual to hear you actually admit to something. Who was he spying for? I didn't kill him. That was Hermes' job.'

'Like that matters.'

Zeus cut in, 'Considering it cost him his head, I would say it matters a great deal.'

'That oh so useful idiot, Hermes, went and confronted him in public and let his tongue fly, nearly exposed our whole plan. I didn't ask questions. His absence was necessary.'

Charon thought back to that incident. Hermes pushing the boy back over the bar. It would appear this was the mess he was giving Hermes a dressing down for the other night, but Robin was already dead by then.

'Okay. So who would you suspect he was working for?' Zeus asked.

'I don't know.'

'I'm sure you can guess.'

'He was a double agent.'

'Who for?' Zeus was standing over him now, elbow to elbow with Odin.

'The Fae would be the most obvious. Snivelling little fool wanted to ingratiate himself and get back in their good books.'

'And the others?' Zeus raised an eyebrow.

Had the Fae sat and watched all this unfolding and done nothing? Had they told the council? Thought Charon.

'Others?'

'You said 'double agent'. You know an awful lot for someone who didn't ask him anything,' Odin said. 'Who else was he working for?'

'That would be us, well, me,' a voice said from the

main doors. It was Ra.

'Guards!' Odin and Zeus shouted together and within moments Ra was surrounded.

'Unhand me and I will tell you what you want to know.'

'You mean you'll gloat, and posture just like when you summoned us all to a meeting in one of my own properties.' Zeus said.

'Yes, well, it's not just me who's sick of this place. I'm not the only one who's had enough of being pushed around by the Fae. We're Gods! We should be running this place, not hiding in holes and trying not to be noticed.'

'Loki and Hermes are working for you?'

'Not exactly. Loki came to me with the suggestion that there might be a way to go home but it would take time to organise. Somebody needed to do something about our current situation. I merely took him up on his offer and agreed with everything he asked in return for his help. I gave him leave to recruit help where needed. Hermes was collateral damage. All he had to do was keep his friend out of my hair. He couldn't even get that right. Don't be too hard on Hermes. If you ask me, just being him is punishment enough.'

'It is not your place to decide our fate or to advise me on how to deal with my people,' Zeus shouted. He strode up to Ra, jaw set and fists clenched.

Ra yawned, 'And yet the only one brave enough to have even tried to stop me is hiding from the both of you with the sword of Damocles hanging over his head.'

A voice from the back chipped in, 'I wondered where I'd left that.' This was answered by quiet snorts of laughter from those who would rather not admit to finding that sort of smart-arsed remark both clever and funny. At least not in public.

Ra paused and waited for the sniggering to subside. 'You think me foolish enough to rely on only one spy? You are all so wonderfully petty and parochial, that I implemented my plans without so much of a whisper of complaint. All bar one.'

'He will be dealt with once we find him.

Insubordination is a serious charge.'

Ra laughed. 'Even now, you cannot allow a subordinate to best you at anything. You had every opportunity to swallow your pride and stop me. Instead you hid and you tried to deflect, and you send servants to find out something you already know.' There were gasps through the room, and Zeus looked thunderstruck, 'Yes, I know about the dragon. You might have stood a chance if you had been able to stop bickering and work together. It's all my plan relied upon and thankfully you did not disappoint.' He smiled but it did not meet his eyes. At that point, Ra reminded Charon of a cobra about to strike. 'What will you do now Zeus, my old friend?'

'You are not my friend.'

'A fact for which I am eternally thankful. You see, I have seen how you treat your friends when it no longer suits your purpose.' He turned to Odin. 'And you? What can we say of Odin? The Wise Old Man? He paid with an eye, but it seems all that did was leave you half blind. Little word of advice: if you are going to start removing your own body parts you should make sure they will grow back.'

Hathor, the goddess who was formed from Ra's eye, and used to spy for Ra found that her place had been taken on her return. She was most displeased. The moral of the story is, when taking any extended time away from home, always lock the door on your way out.

'Your taunts will not get a rise out of me, boy!'

'Boy? I was three thousand years old before you had even been dreamed up!'

'So much for great age bringing great wisdom. Your scheme has doomed us all!' shouted Zeus.

'True, there have been a few unforeseen consequences, but none of that will matter once we are home.'

'Will we all get home, Ra?' Zeus asked, 'Because from what I hear, your plan was a non-transferable single seat ticket.'

There were gasps through the room. Charon realised then that some of these people were hearing this for the first time. He wondered how many had secretly rooted for Ra and his plan to go home.

'Ah. Yes, I thought you might have heard that by now. Pity. I'd hoped to keep that quiet. Some clever deduction, and well-remembered lore on the part of your man. What was his name again?'

'Charon. What of him?'

'In short, had he not been such an insufferable busy body on your behalf, you would not have found out, or should I say been reminded of, half of what you know today. You should thank him by the way. You can't buy loyalty like that.'

'Reminded of?'

'Have you two forgotten so soon?' Ra laughed, but there was no warmth. His voice had become harsh and sibilant. With outstretched arms, he addressed the room. 'We are here today because you are both cowards who, when faced with enemies you could not defeat, saw fit to lock them away, banish or enslave them, I merely took advantage of a situation that you two created for yourselves, and I for one cannot wait to see what you do next.' He inclined his head in a mocking gesture of respect, shook his head, and left the room.

It took a few moments for Ra's admission to sink in. Hermes and Loki had believed his lies because they wanted to go home. That desire could be forgiven. He could even sympathise a little. What he could not forgive was the fact that they had both been willing to take innocent lives to get there. This was why the mortals had stopped believing and worshipping. Why the stories had faded, and their friends with them. The mortals had grown tired of them playing with their lives just to score points against each other, or even because they felt slighted or bored. Phaedra and Hippolytus were not the only victims of divine hubris. *We deserve to be stuck here, living as they do. It is our penance for so many centuries of torment and bloodshed,* Charon thought, *we left the door open for someone like Yahweh to sneak in and take over, and we were all too busy squabbling to notice until it was too late.*

And here they were again. Repeating the same patterns which got them banished the first time. Dionysus was right. Trouble was, if they couldn't beat back the united Titan and Giant threat, it wasn't just banishment they had to worry about and it was more than just the gods who would suffer.

It didn't take long for Zeus and Odin to agree to a temporary truce, if only so they could wipe that smug grin off Ra's face. They decided they would not sit and wait for their enemies to strike. A field of battle was agreed upon, and even Ares agreed to cooperate. He seemed to hold respect for warriors whose only care in battle was to die with a sword in their hand. Vigrid Plain, it was decided, was not a practical venue for the final battle, not least because it was on the wrong side of a barrier they couldn't cross. The Rye Marsh, it was decided, was a sound spot as it had little in the way of high ground and the wet flood plain would be a tactical advantage. There was a fair amount of grumbling, on the part of Odin's men, that Ragnarök should not be taking place on a flooded football pitch. Asclepius was charged with organising medics to help patch up any mortals that were stupid enough to be walking their dogs across a battlefield. It would be impossible to keep this one quiet and not alert the council, so Zeus and Odin decided they might as well do it out in the open and give a few mad poets a thing or two to write about.

CHAPTER 26

Ragnarök?

It was the eve of battle. So far, Charon had managed to resist turning his phone back on. The pleading text messages from Zeus claiming all was forgiven, were not holding sway with him. Zeus knew where he was. If he wanted to speak to him that badly, he could come down and half-apologise in person, thank you very much. In a way, he felt vindicated by what Ra had said, though he would never admit that self-satisfied twit was right about anything. He stopped himself. Was his animosity toward Ra because Ra was right, or was it because he was just a bit of a prat? He settled on the idea that it was probably a bit of both and decided to leave it at that.

He looked at the clock. It said, five pm. All was definitely not well. Erick had popped by over the last couple of days with some spare clothes, boots, an sword, a shield and an eyeglass helmet, so Charon would not be recognised by anyone. Zeus might be pleading for Charon to return to the fold, now a welcome hero but Odin had not said a word. Erick had reasoned that nobody would expect him to turn up at all, let alone looking like a Viking. Anyone that wanted to kill him would be looking out for a grumpy old Greek with bad posture and flat feet. He'd had to practice with the shield. He hadn't realised how heavy they could be and if he was seen to be struggling with it he might as well be wearing a neon sign saying, 'Does not belong!' He rubbed his sore shoulder.

One thing which seemed odd was that a few days after the war had been officially declared, Ra, Loki and Hermes had all vanished. What made this even more odd was that no attempt had been made to find them. Charon had contemplated going to investigate but a handwritten message addressed to him arrived, expressly forbidding him from getting involved. That was weird too. It had been sealed with old fashioned wax, as if out of time. If it had not been for the fact that the wax was pink, the stamp would have looked even more official. Even so, he dared not argue with it, even though it was on forget-me-not scented paper which had small pink peonies printed in the corners. Nor was the letter signed. He'd racked his brains for days trying to think of what those flowers reminded him of. So much had happened in too little time and it was all just squashed into one bitter, leaden lump in the pit of his stomach.

More orders from person or persons unknown. When were they going to stop playing games with him? He'd had enough. If he survived tomorrow he would move away. Somewhere they couldn't find him. He got out his broom to start cleaning up but didn't know why he was bothering. It would take a minor miracle to keep the foyer clean. The bin bag he'd taped over the broken window had helped to keep some of the dead leaves out but did nothing for the draft and the wind was making it rattle and rustle. As he swept up he thought about the last few weeks. Hermes' betrayal. Having to hide from Zeus and Odin. He hadn't asked for any of this and it all boiled down to him eavesdropping on one meeting. In a fit of temper, he spun around and hurled the broom at the back wall as hard as he could, hoping to hit the dreadful plastic plant and smash the pot. At the very least it would give him an excuse to sling the horrid thing out.

'That is quite enough of that, Mr Charon.' It was The Nurse. She had caught it in one hand and stood with the other on her hip. 'I take it that it wasn't my note that has put you in such a foul mood.'

'What? How?' Charon spluttered. 'The doors are locked. How did you get in?'

'Oh, let's just say I have an access all areas pass. You and I need a little chat.'

'Your note?'

'Well you'd turned off your phone.'

'You sent the text messages?'

'All bar the first. The Fae were worried you would get yourself killed or worse, foul up our investigation. You'd stumbled in at a very delicate point. It took a lot of persuasion to let me keep using you.'

Realisation dawned. How else could she have known so much? It wasn't Zeus who had called that ambulance, they had been watching him. 'You're with the Council.'

'Well-reasoned, Mr Charon. I am one of their

representatives.'

'Don't you lot normally come in threes?'

'Who says I am not?' She smiled. 'Tea?' A familiar tea tray appeared on the table he had been sweeping round. The nurse sat down and began heaping sugar into one of the cups. After six, she stirred what Charon suspected bore closer resemblance to syrup than tea and took a sip.

'You could have told me.'

'Sadly, that is not the case. If I had told you, what would you have done?'

'Before he tried to kill me I would have told Hermes. But afterwards? I don't know.'

'It wasn't safe for you to know. Especially after what happened to poor Robin.'

'He was working for you? Loki was telling the truth.'

'He does that. It really can be quite the annoyance. This investigation has been going on for a long time. Years in fact. The Fae loaned Robin to us. All that stuff about his exile was a cover story so he could get close to Loki without raising suspicion, but we needed to know who he was working with on your side. Loki couldn't have released the Titans alone. You gave us a way to keep an eye on him.'

'But Odin knew what was going on. *He* told me.'

'And you told Hermes. Who went and told Loki that they were in danger of being found out. Did you not wonder why he disappeared?'

'But that night at the paint factory, they knocked him out? Odin's men held him hostage?'

'Odin's men found him out cold on the roof with his phone in camera mode. They thought he was with you. That meeting was called to flush out whoever released the Ice Giants. When you set off the wards it created a diversion for Loki and a few others to slip away. Which, in a way, achieved their goal. They were conspicuous by their absence. We suspect that one of Loki's followers knocked him out to keep him from saying something… inconvenient.

'Of course. But leaving a meeting isn't proof of conspiracy. It only means they don't want to be at the meeting.'

'Exactly. And what did you do when he did suddenly make himself scarce?'

'I carried on looking.'

The nurse beamed, 'Correct. You carried on looking. You'd made a promise to do something, at very great risk to yourself, and were determined to carry out that promise.'

'I made a bit of a hash of it if I remember?'

'You'll learn. That prophecy of Zoë's helped us persuade the Fae that their level of caution was dangerous. They have since left us alone to get on with it and we have progressed in leaps and bounds, thanks in part to you.'

'But anyone could…'

'No, anyone couldn't. You could speak to Zoë on her level. That girl is extremely shrewd. She would have seen through me in an instant and sent me on my way with a flea in my ear. We needed someone who could get close to the situation without revealing that we knew what was going on, especially considering how hard they had tried to keep this all from us. But I have no real authority over her, or anyone else.' she said

'And Robin?'

'Robin will be missed but he knew the risks and he sacrificed his life so the investigation could carry on. Nobody has to work for us.'

Charon went to pick up his cup but hesitated, 'Why do I get the feeling that this is leading somewhere else?' He wanted to know exactly what it would mean

She sighed. 'Very well. The Council would like to retain your services.'

'For how long?'

'For as long as you feel comfortable. I told you, nobody has to work for us. You don't have to answer now. Sleep on it and tell me tomorrow.'

'You do remember what's happening tomorrow, right?'

The nurse just smiled and sipped her tea.

* * *

The next day was sunny and bright. It somehow felt wrong to have a battle on such a day, but even they couldn't control the weather: At least, not anymore. Charon hadn't slept well but figured that if he survived, he could sleep for a week. As he approached the battlefield he noticed that two trestle tables had been set up to one side and were laden with blue face and body paint. This was a less expensive, far less toxic, alternative to the traditional woad. Besides which, woad was out of season. One of them was bowing in the middle. He considered giving it a go but realised he might be recognised. He spotted Erick in the lines and went to join him.

'Thought for a moment that you'd be late.'

'What me? I couldn't let my people face this lot alone. Has Zeus turned up?'

'Yes. He's over there being painted. Figured that if it works for us, it was worth a go. It's a shame we couldn't get any woad. This stuff feels like cheating.

And it itches.'

'What's that over there?

'Where?'

Charon pointed toward the river and the woods, 'There.'

'Oh. That's Ra's barque.'

Charon was impressed. It looked completely out of place on an English boating river but the golden vessel gleamed in the spring sun. He could see men, muscular and stripped to the waist, working on board, and heard the linen sails rippling and snapping in the wind. Perhaps the most impressive part of it being there was the fact that the only waterway to that part of the river was underground, and the only way off it was down a waterfall with a weir at the top and a sixteen-foot drop to an ankle-deep brook at the bottom. Never mind the canopy of trees overhanging that part of the river. Ra was showing off.

'What's he doing?'

'Waiting.' Erick yawned.

'What? He started all this. This is what he wanted!'

'Why do you think he brought the boat? He reckons we're going to lose.'

'We can't let that happen.' Charon was determined he wasn't going back home. Even if Ra's plan worked, and there was no guarantee it would, the idea of going back to life on the Styx was no more appealing now than it had been when he first heard Ra's plan. *But then, this plan was never meant for us, this has always been about Ra.* Hermes had helped him. More than that, Hermes had lied to his face, tried to put him off getting involved, and then tried to kill him. Charon decided that if nothing else was achieved that day, he was going to kill Hermes. He wasn't proud of it but he still felt it. He'd seen the carnage that a cycle of revenge could cause. During Troy, Charon had to consider taking on extra help just to cope with the traffic over the river. From Phaedra and Hippolytus, to Orestes avenging Agamemnon by killing his mother and her lover, revenge had done nothing but temporarily sate one person's rage after another, after another.

Orestes had not been quite so keen to avenge his

poor sister, Iphigenia, against their father. She had been sacrificed to Artemis after her father had killed one of her sacred animals, and Agamemnon found his ships stuck in becalmed seas. Nor was he interested in the fact that after his father had used that wind to spend ten years besieging Troy because his brother's wife had run off with someone with a bigger palace - leaving Clytemnestra behind to run the palace and bring up their surviving kids by herself - he then spent another ten years gallivanting around the Mediterranean with Odysseus. To add insult to injury, when he finally returned, he installed his new girlfriend in the palace and paraded her in front of his wife. Unsurprisingly, Clytemnestra decided she'd had quite enough of this nonsense, thank you very much. Too bad Cassandra didn't see that poison coming. Then again, even if she had said anything nobody would have believed her. Notwithstanding, the Erinyes had a thing or two to say on the subject.

'I don't think it will, but even so, the coward has apparently been taking lessons from Lord Stanley's Big Book of Battlefield Tactics.'[4]

---

[4] This roughly boils down to sitting on the side-lines until you see who's winning, then backing the winning side.

'Must be.'

Erick, suddenly spat in disgust. 'Loki!'

'Where?'

'On the front lines. He still thinks they are going to send him home. Has he learned nothing about Giants?'

Loki was on the front line with Fenrir by his side but Hel was not with him. He wondered if she was in Odin's lines? He remembered that Ragnarök would only occur if certain conditions were in place. If she was not there, what would happen? The enemy lines stretched from one side of the field to the other and were at least twenty men deep. It was made up of gods, demons, ghouls and all manner of other supernatural beings, lined up and ready to fight to go home or die in the attempt. Some had come from the other side of the world. The Greek-Norse side easily matched them in number and were taking it in turns to shout insults at the enemy.

'Loki wouldn't really be welcome here, would he?'

'He would not. Odin wants him flayed alive,

destiny be damned. Trying to manipulate fate is a big fat no-no. Oh, and the Council have told him that he is not to harm you. He's now under a Council audit and been called to a private interview to explain himself. I wouldn't be surprised if Zeus has too.'

Charon said nothing. He hoped the Council did tear a few strips off Zeus. He had tried to throw Charon to the wolves just for knowing too much about what he wasn't doing. He'd followed his orders and done as he'd promised but the only acknowledgement he'd got was from Ra, and only because it was an easy dig at Zeus. Maybe he should join the Council. It would be worth telling Zeus just to see the look on his face when he quit being a doorman in an empty building.

Then came the call to attention. Zeus and Odin marched up and down giving the expected inspiring speeches. Nobody was impressed as most of the soldiers knew exactly what had been going on by now, and newcomers had no doubt been filled in. Odin and Zeus had tried to hide their parts in it, but by hiding they had exposed themselves. Not through deliberate action, but by ignoring the rot as it spread. All the suspicion and mistrust which had led them to be banished was still there, lurking under the surface. Charon looked at his watch. Since the call to muster, they'd been wittering on for at least ten minutes, and by the look of it even the giants were bored. Then came something nobody expected, the pair shook hands.

Ymir bellowed across the field, 'Odin, have you finished talking false hope into your men yet? Time is marching and I have a world to make comfortable.' His men laughed.

Ymir was huge. He stood at about three times the height of Odin and Zeus, and they were not small men. The Titans matched the giants in both size and in number. Were it not for the fact that the Greeks and Vikings out-numbered them, they would not have stood a chance. The Titans had every right to be angry. They had been locked away just for existing. Mind you, Cronos had been so terrified of his successors that he ate five of his own children just to avoid them. Zeus had been warned that this would happen and now they would all pay the price. Numbers alone would not save them all.

'Line commanders! Give your orders!' Odin yelled.

'Shield! Wall!' The order went up from each end of the lines, and as one both sides stood with their shields raised and locked in row upon row of overlapping limewood. 'Weapons!' the crashing of weapons against shields echoed around the field. 'Archers at the ready!' Two ranks of archers nocked their arrows, drew their bows and aimed for the sky. One of the axemen began to mark time and was soon joined by the rest. 'First rank! Fire!'

At last Odin raised his sword and gave the call to advance. It happened slowly at first. The banging of axes and swords was deafening but it created a numbing rhythm. Charon could shut away the worries of tomorrow and do what must be done today. He kept his eye on the now advancing line of the enemy and kept marching. Gone was the rage of yesterday evening. Now, he was just determined to protect the world he had called home for so many centuries. He liked his life and he did not want to go back to the Underworld.

He did not hear the call to charge but, suddenly, they were moving forward at an astonishing rate. Erick had joined a comrade in taking down one of the smaller Ice Giants who now had several spears hanging out of his chest and was roaring in pain and rage. As Charon rushed past he took a chance and slashed his sword across the giant's back as hard as he could. The giant fell face first into the mud. Blood splattered across his face where the helmet did not cover but he kept going. He had never considered himself a killer but this fight was a them or us situation. The battlefield had no place for pacifists. Charon was numb to the noise and the danger. All he knew was that he had to find Hermes. Anything else was a distraction. Once he had dealt with Hermes…

It was chaos. Blood and mud caked his arms and legs and made it almost impossible to recognise anybody. He rushed past where Loki and Fenrir were locked in combat against Ares, who had already taken down Ephilates, and Dionysus had taken on Alcyoneus, a giant with a terrible reputation. Its long hair, which appeared to have had sharp stone chips sewn into the ends, flew out behind it as it spun and dipped to duck the arrows being fired from both the Greek and the Viking ranks. Charon had not been paying full attention, and one of the strands struck him across his shield arm, tearing the flimsy linen and cutting deeply. Hera and Athena were also fighting furiously and as he passed them, Athena blocked a club which was heading toward his head. He nodded his gratitude before continuing his search for Hermes.

It already felt like the battle had been going on for hours. His injured arm throbbed and blood soaked his sleeve. He tried to ignore the pain and the noise as he dodged Greeks, Vikings, Titans and Giants, arrows, rocks and bits of his 'allies'. Finally, he came upon Hermes. He was fighting hand to hand with Artemis – never a woman to get on the wrong side of. He saw Ares, who had now dispatched Fenrir, pinning Hermes with his spear, 'Stop!' Charon screamed as he tore off his blood-spattered helmet and retrieved his sword. 'Hermes is mine!'.

'Charon!? What the hell are you doing here, you idiot? Go home before you get yourself killed!' Ares bellowed back. He moved into attack again.

'I said he's mine!' Charon's heart pounded as he turned his ire on Ares. He remembered what Erick had told him about how to get past a spearman. He had to get the shield boss over the top of the spear and force the point down. Then he could slide up the shaft and take him down. Erick had made him practice for a whole day and if he had to, he'd use it. Through gritted teeth, he snarled 'He tried to kill me in my own home! I demand satisfaction!'

Ares, lowered his spear and shook his head, 'Wow, that's low. Dude, look, it's your call, but have you ever fought before?' He held an arm out to stop Charon from charging in.

'It doesn't matter! I know enough for what I need.'

'If you need help—' He tore a strip from his own cloak and bound Charon's arm. Everyone else was too busy fighting to take any notice of them.

'I won't! Just keep other people out of it. He dies by my hand or none!'

Ares looked at him as if seeing him for the first time and nodded approvingly, 'I don't know how much time you've been spending around them, but it looks like someone's grown some stones. Have at him.'

Charon nodded and, feeling no inclination to announce his presence, charged, hitting Hermes on his left side and sent him sprawling in the mud. 'Get up and fight, traitor!'

Artemis, stunned by this sudden interruption, attempted to re-join the fray. Ares took her arm and pulled her away. A simple shake of his head was enough to tell her to leave this one to Charon. The goddess of the hunt needed no verbal explanation. Instead, she and Ares stood either side of them as Hermes and Charon circled each other, trading blow for blow, each holding their ground.

'You think yourself a warrior now?' Hermes scoffed.

'Last time I only had a golf club. Just think what I can do with this,' and swung his sword at Hermes who deflected it with his shield. He went in again for an upper cut but Hermes again deflected it.

'Not much by the look of it.' Hermes swung his own sword in a series of blows which were obviously an attempt to send Charon off balance. Erick's patient training kicked in and he was able to block them while putting in some of his own. A lucky strike allowed Charon to bury his sword in Hermes' shield arm. It fell in the mud with a sickening squelch. Hermes screamed from pain and shock.

'Don't bet on it.' Charon charged Hermes again, this time striking him in the chest with the edge of his shield. Hermes dropped to his knees like a stone. Charon circled again as Hermes clutched his chest with his remaining arm, gasping. He could have struck then but he wanted Hermes to know it was coming. He wanted him to suffer; to know he was going to die. Killing him fast would not sate his rage. Charon did not like this side of himself, but he felt powerful. Blue lightning rippled up and down his arms and over his hands. Blue flames danced in his eyes, and reflected back from Hermes' who, still on his knees, was either unwilling or unable to move.

Good men have no need to gloat. They will just do what must be done. Without a word, Charon swung his sword from right to left. It passed through Hermes' neck without resistance, sending blood spraying and his head tumbling into the mud, landing face down. Hermes' body, now lacking the means to remain upright, slumped forward. Charon looked at the head for a moment then stamped on it hard until the mud consumed it. Turning back to Ares and Artemis who stared wide-eyed at what he had done, he said, 'Where's Loki?'

* * *

The battle lasted hours, but they were only able to round up a few of the remaining Titans and Giants and lock them away again until they could think of a way to properly neutralise them. Those they caught went willingly for the most part but a great number had fled as soon as they realised the battle was lost. Shipping containers had been found to contain them until a more permanent solution could be found. Charon stormed off the battlefield after that decision was made public. They were making the same stupid mistakes all over again. *Why did they never learn?* Locking them up had given them a reason to hate the gods. It had bred the animosity that had brought them there in the first place, and now they were going to let it grow stronger. Loki and Ra had vanished so he hadn't been able to send him to join Hermes but there was time. There was always time.

He opened his front door and sighed. He hadn't been home in days and the place was still as he'd left it after the fight with Hermes. He leaned his shield and sword against the wall in the hall. After the display on the battlefield, Odin and Erick had insisted he keep them. He went into the kitchen where he found two bags of shopping on the table with a peony printed note pinned to it.

'I have been feeding the Hellbeast. She asked me to tell you that her name is Susan, not Stupid Cat, and can you please get some more of the cat food with jelly as the stuff in gravy is a devil to wash out of her coat. Milk is in the fridge.'

Charon smiled. It was the first normal thing that had happened in weeks. *Bath, tea, bed,* he thought. He'd deal with the mess in the morning. Flicking the radio on as he waited for the kettle to boil, he considered the Council's offer of a position. It beat being a doorman. With tea in hand, he went upstairs and soaked in the bath. Every muscle was complaining and he wanted to wash Hermes' blood off. He felt tainted by it. It was like being soaked in treachery. On the upside, people might think twice before assuming he was a doormat in future.

An hour or so later, he came back downstairs for more tea and saw the light on the answer machine, the one thing which hadn't been destroyed in the fight, was flashing. That was weird. Nobody called his landline, let alone left messages. He'd only got one because he'd read somewhere that it's what humans did. He hit play and went into the kitchen to boil the kettle.

Ra's voice came out of the machine and Charon shuddered, 'Good evening, Charon. I thought I would drop you a quick line to tell you that, in payment for costing me everything I have worked so hard to achieve, I have taken your wife. Say hello, my dear.' He heard the sounds of a struggle on the other end.

'You'll pay for this, you bast...' There was a muffled scuffle in the background and an angry yell of pain from one of her captors.

'She certainly has spirit, doesn't she? If you want to see her in one piece again, you'll come to the paint factory as soon as you get this message.' The message ended.

Without waiting for the kettle or turning off the radio, Charon picked up his keys and his sword and left the house. As the door slammed shut, the DJ on the radio announced the next tune and Rhinestone Cowboy began playing to the empty house.

Rules of The Council and the Conditions of The Settlement of the Gods.

A. H. Johnstone

The Rules of the Council.

The council are a group of divine judiciaries. They were appointed by the Sidhe courts because they were the only beings capable of keeping a lid on the others. They *do not* include the oracles or seers because, though they were permitted to pass over from the Underworld as attendants, they were not seen as objective enough to be a part of the council.

1. No single Pantheon will rule over the others.
2. No god may act to prevent or undo the work of another[5].
3. No member of any pantheon may act in aggression against either the mortals or each other.

---

[5] This little treasure was brought with them before they crossed over. It probably caused more trouble than it cured, and more than one hero fell afoul of warring gods using mortals as pawns to harm their rivals. Poor Phaedra was not the only victim of Aphrodite's jealousy and rage.

> *a. Grievances must be brought to the attention of the council for arbitration.*
>
> *b. The council has the final word in all disputes.*

4. Gods may interact socially, but all official cross-pantheon agreements and meetings must include at least two representatives from The Council to ensure that the above rules are observed and adhered to.

5. Representatives of the Council have no power to act on the behalf of the Gods. They act only to pass information and see that The Council is obeyed.

6. The Oracles must operate only under license and only insofar as the council deems appropriate. They fall under the jurisdiction of Wadjet.

7. Predicting the outcome of mortal wars is forbidden.

8. Using predictions for personal gain is also prohibited.

9. On no account is Dionysus allowed to bet on anything!

A. H. Johnstone

Conditions of Settlement[6]

Here is the list of conditions that the gods were made to submit to in exchange for freedom to pass into the mortal world, after being thrown from their own.

1. The gods agree to put past differences behind them. Warring will not be tolerated. All new differences must be mediated by The Council as soon as they arise. If the Council cannot reach a decision, The Sidhe Courts will have the final word.
2. Mortal followers are **not** to be used as pawns to settle arguments.

---

[6] As laid down by the Sidhe Courts. This is one of the few times the Dark and Light Courts of the Fae have ever acted in agreement.

3. The gods agree to remain in human form at all times. Messing about pretending to be swans, or strange ethereal voices in caves, is not encouraged. Impersonating others (mortal or otherwise) will be met with severe punishment[7].
4. It is forbidden to use your powers against mortals for any reason.
5. No attempt to influence the mortal population will be tolerated. For this reason, the Gods agree not to run for public office in any capacity.
6. The gods will do nothing to risk public exposure of their existence, or the existence of other supernatural beings. A low-profile lifestyle is expected of all.

---

[7] This was mostly aimed at Zeus.

7. The gods agree that they will do nothing to extend their lives. Once their stories have faded from the mortal land, so must the gods. Attempts to artificially keep their stories, or rekindle belief in the world of man, is forbidden.

8. The gods agree that the Head gods remain responsible for policing their subordinates. Above them is The Council appointed by the Fae courts.

9. If one of the Head gods is found to have breached these conditions their discipline is to be determined by The Council.

10. If one of their subordinates are found guilty of the same, their Head must report it to the council for them to decide punishment.

11. Apocalyptic omens should be reported to the Sidhe Courts. Do not attempt to deal with these alone.

A. H. Johnstone

Upcoming...

A. H. Johnstone

The Bet

Chapter 1

The Styx - 312 CE

Charon woke with a start. Waves were lapping at his ankles. This was very wrong. This should not be happening. This meant that that stupid dog had let people in. Again. The Styx famously didn't have waves. Or a current. Or wind. So what the Euripides was going on in his river? He had one job to do and gods darn it, he was going to do it. *Enough is enough!* He thought, and stepped onto his raft, stopping briefly to wring out the hem of his robe over the edge.

He punted to the other side of the river, eyes

flaring bright blue, and muttering to himself about idiot heroes and their mad ideas. *If this is Orpheus again, I'll drown him myself!* He thought, though this was, strictly speaking, not allowed. It was Charon's job to ferry the dead, not create them. Last year Orpheus had spent a week down here sulking and moping around because he had failed to follow instructions, and you would not have believed the noise. Charon didn't have ears but after three days he'd been driven to stuff where they would have been with marsh mud. To this day Charon would blush at the memory of the language Orpheus was yelling when he was eventually chucked out. Considering he didn't have a face, blushing was an achievement.

When he pulled up to the other pontoon he was very much surprised to find Hermes and Dionysus in the river as naked as the day they were manifested, stinking drunk, and frolicking with a couple of nymphs. *Why is it always nymphs?* 'Oi! You two, idiots. Get out of there right now!'

'Sshhh... Hermes, i'ss Charon.' There was a lot of splashing and, *oh gods, giggling*, as Dionysus and Hermes tried to help each other out of the river; falling over one another in an attempt to get to the edge.

'Are you quite finished?'

'Nearly there… *hic*… old chap.' Called Hermes.

'If we schtay really quiet, do you reckon he'll bugger off?' slurred Dionysus.

'Nah, mate, he's looking right at us. Pass the horn, I need another drink.' Hermes belched loudly.

Dionysus patted himself down, forgetting he was naked, then looked back over to the nymphs, 'left it with the girls. They're…' he flailed an arm roughly to where four -when he could have sworn they only brought two – were swapping two identical and slightly out of focus horns between them, 'they're over there.' He continued swaying toward the shore.

Charon was standing on the dock with his arms folded and tapping his foot, 'Get a move on. What do you think this is, a pleasure beach? Have some respect. And look at the state you've left it in!' Charon stretched out a skeletal arm to indicate the tunics and sandals left strewn across the river bank.

'Calm down, Charon.' Dionysus paused to belch

before speaking again, 'You'll get frown lines...' He and Hermes fell back into the river in fits of laughter.

'Oh, very funny. Do you have any clue what Hades will do if he catches you two messing around down here with them?' Charon said, pointing at the nymphs.

'Whatever it is, it won't be good.' This was a new voice and they all jumped before turning to find Yahweh, Gabriel, Baal and Azrael, standing about five meters from the water's edge.

Oh, great, thought Hermes, *that lot*. 'Get lost, Yahweh,' said Hermes, swaying as he made his way back up to the bank to get clothes, 'you're lowering the tone.'

'From where I'm standing, I would have a job.' Yahweh smirked, and ran his hand through his greasy dark curls. 'Besides which, it's not the tone you're worried about. It's the competition.'

'You? Competition?' Dionysus had joined them on the riverbank again, this time with a naked nymph on each arm, 'don't make me laugh. You're barely five centuries old. And yeah, I've heard all the rubbish you've been spouting to the mortals about being the 'One True God'. He dressed himself and tucked his horn in his belt.

'Does the little godling think he can convince the mortals he's the big scary now?' Hermes taunted, and ruffled Yahweh's hair. He then wiped the grease off on Yahweh's tunic in disgust. 'Listen boy, you're a nothing. Even the Romans have been ignoring your lot for decades. It's gotten to the point where they're making their own martyrs. Until you get a decent following out there, you'll stay a nothing in here, and as Zeus is keeping a very close eye on what you minor pests are up to, it's going to be a warm day in the Underworld before you get that.'

Dionysus nudged him, 'Diocletian does give them some grief.'

'Oh, right. Forgot about him.'

It was at this point that Charon chipped in, 'Sorry to burst your bubble but Diocletian is old news.'

'What? How do you know what's going on up there?'

'I don't. I know what goes on down here, and I can tell you first hand that Diocletian has been dead for several months.'

'You sure?'

'I ferried him myself.' Said Charon.

Yahweh and his gang started to laugh, 'You clowns don't have a clue what your own followers are up to, and you have the front to mock me? Last time I checked, I have not one but two religions following me.'

'That are essentially the same...' Hermes muttered under his breath.

'Just admit it, you're too old and too out of touch to get what we're about.'

'I get what you're about, puppy,' said Dionysus, 'and I don't much like it. Gods take care of their own affairs.'

'Really? Is that what you call persecuting members of rival cults because Zeus won't let you fight each other?'

'It's just how it's done.' said Hermes. 'You've not seen the destruction when gods fight directly. You're too young to understand.'

'I call it cowardly.' Said Yahweh, 'Things are going to change around here, starting with you lot.'

'Yeah, out with the old, in with the new, hey, Yahweh?' said Baal.

'That's right.'

Hermes, Charon and Dionysus just looked at each other, and then collapsed into a heap of laughing bodies. After several minutes on their knees crying with laughter. Well, Hermes and Dionysus were crying: Charon's ability to cry was severely limited by his total lack of tear ducts.

Yahweh stood with his gang looking like he was about to explode with rage. His hands were clenched into fists and his lips were pressed tight, 'Laugh all you like, it won't change the inevitable. You'll all pay for laughing at me!' Yahweh screamed and kicked sand in their faces.

The laughter stopped abruptly, and Dionysus shot

to his feet, 'Hey! You can pack that in now you spoiled little brat.' He shoved the young god who fell back into Gabriel, and they landed in a heap.

Azrael and Baal stepped forward and shoved back but Dionysus had a slight weight advantage. Being outnumbered didn't seem to bother him either. Baal was taking a fighting stance.

'Go on, Di, smack him in the face!' Hermes shouted while washing sand from his face and hair.

The Nymphs had retreated to the safety of the dock to watch and were sitting on the edge, dangling their feet in the water and placing bets on who they thought would hit the ground first.

Dionysus raised his eyebrows, cocked his head, shrugged, and then suddenly headbutted Baal hard on the nose, sending him flailing back into Azrael. As most who have ever tried headbutting someone can attest to, this is generally not a good idea. Dionysus did put Baal out of the fight, but he also very nearly knocked himself out. He staggered back swaying and, holding his forehead, fell back into the river. Much to Hermes' amusement. Eventually Hermes heaved his friend out of the water and gave him a sharp slap to bring him around.

Baal's nose was bleeding profusely, and his chest was streaked with muddy water and blood. Not that this was much worse than he normally looked. Most of the time he looked like he'd spent a week being dragged behind a dung cart and smelled about half as nice.

'Hermes, get off me. I need to finish this.'

'Nah, mate, you've had enough. Look, when I said smack him in the face, I didn't mean with your own. Your eyes are all weird.' Said Hermes.

'YAHWEH! You worm, stop hiding behind your flunkies and face me like a man!' Dionysus bellowed, pushing past Hermes. 'Yahweh!'

'What do you want, old man?'

'This is settled now. I suggest a wager.'

Oh gods, thought Hermes.

'Keep talking.'

'It's no secret that we're all sick of you and your

gang of grinning idiots, strutting around like you're the next big thing. You're not. Never will be.'

'Is this going somewhere?' Yahweh stepped just that little bit too close to Dionysus for comfort.

Why does he do that? And the staring? Dionysus wanted to shudder, he could at least take a bath every now and then, the greasy little toad.

'Well?'

Dionysus, held his ground, 'I bet that you don't have the wherewithal to convert even one human by yourself.'

'Before I go off and prove you wrong, which human and what's at stake?' Yahweh asked, suspicious. There was a hint of a glint in his eye that told Hermes that Dionysus was playing right into his hands.

'Suddenly cautious, are we? Hardly the stance of a great leader...' Hermes jeered.

'Shut up, Herm!' Dionysus turned back to Yahweh 'Let's say, oh, how about Constantine?'

Yahweh shrugged, 'Fair enough. The stakes?'

'If you fail, Yahweh, you will be banished to the mortal realm until the end of time.'

'And if we win?'

'We? You're in this on your own, sunshine.' Said Hermes.

'Fine. What's in it for me?'

'Control of the immortal realms—'

'NO!' Yelled Charon and Hermes together.

'Done!' shouted Yahweh and grabbed Dionysus's hand to seal the deal before anyone could qualify it!

To Be Continued...

A.H. Johnstone

A. H. Johnstone

Notes and references to the more obscure deities.

---

[i] Also known as the Spinners in Norse Mythology. These three goddesses lived at the bottom of Yggdrasil guarding the well, Urdar, from which they watered the world tree to preserve it. They were believed to preside over the fates of both gods and men. Previously there was only one but two were later added. Urdhr (Past), Verdhandi (Present), and Skuld (Future) control fate by carving rune staves and casting lots.

[ii] Greek Philosophers argued that the Promethean creation of man was not the same as the unknown and flawed version of earth-born man that was partially destroyed by Zeus. Refer to Hesiod's Five Ages of Man.

[iii] Reference is to the Deucalionian Flood

[iv] The Battle of the Milvian Bridge took place between the Roman Emperors Constantine I and Maxentius on October 28, 312. The victory led him to convert to Christianity, and with him the rest of the Roman Empire.

[v] The Tower is commonly interpreted as meaning danger, crisis, sudden change, destruction, higher learning, and liberation. It is also a blessing in disguise Change, albeit forceful change is being thrust upon you now and though it may feel like it is happening against your will, you need to remember that this is for

your own good. Change is the only way to unfold all the hidden, until now, possibilities of the 'gold in the Shadow'

[vi] Protector goddess associated with Sekhmet and Mut. Known to the Greek world as Buto. Patron and protector of Lower Egypt prior to unification with Upper Egypt. Had her own oracle in Per-Wadjet and is thought to have been the cult responsible for transmitting oracular tradition to Greece. Her symbols were the Sun disc as displayed on the crown of the royal family, and the serpent. Sometimes shown coiled around the head of Ra to act as his protection. Another common depiction is a serpent coiled around a papyrus stem.

She was closely associated with Hathor and other early deities bearing characteristics of mother goddesses (Mut and Naunet). The connection with Hathor also associates her with Horus. Like many other traditions, she was absorbed into the cult of Ra in her capacity as protector, not least in the belief that she was able to send fire against the enemies of Ra, earning her the title 'Lady of Flame.

After Lower and Upper Egypt were reunited, her association with Sekhmet led to Wadjet's diminution as Sekhmet was believed to be the more powerful of the two goddesses. Sekhmet was seen as the Avenger of Wrongs or the Scarlet Lady (in reference to bloodlust) and also depicted with the sun-disc.

Made in the USA
Columbia, SC
02 February 2018